RETURN OF THE BAD BOY

BAD BOYS OF THE BAYOU

ERIN NICHOLAS

AUTHOR'S NOTE

I've been published for over a decade and have written a lot of books in that time. I actually don't know how many. I've counted a few times before but there are short stories and novellas, bonus material, things that have gone out of print, or been re-worked... and I don't know how to count all of that. I usually say, "over fifty books" and figure that's safe.

But in all of that vagueness there are a few things that have become what I call my "orphans" over the years. Books and stories that don't really *belong* anywhere specific anymore. I was first published with Samhain Publishing which has since closed its doors, and all of those books came back to me, including stand-alone stories that didn't connect with anything else. I've also had some really amazing opportunities to participate in various projects and events and series for which I've written a story (or stories) and I've enjoyed them all! But projects end, and opportunities shift. So, over the years, projects, series, and publishers have come and gone. But the stories are still alive and well. They just don't really *fit* anywhere.

So I finally decided that I needed to give them a home. And a new chance to meet readers! They needed a new place to live. But I needed to put them all together and give them a connection to one another since they didn't have other connections.

And, where else would I make this new home than Louisiana?

Now I couldn't just bring these people (some of whom I've known since before I was published!) to Autre, the home of my other Louisiana books. They don't quite fit there. They have a different vibe. They came from a little different Erin Nicholas. Not totally different, of course. My voice and style have always been pretty consistent.

But these stories are a little grittier. More emotional. The people have a little more baggage than the Boys (and girls) of the Bayou or the people of Boys of the Bayou Gone Wild. They're also a little dirtier. There's always open-door sex scenes in my books, but in Bad, Louisiana, there are just more of them. These books just have a little different feel. And they needed their own home. Their own place to live and be what they are rather than trying to fit into something else.

So, I present to you Bad, Louisiana. A collection of books that have existed in Erin Nicholas world for a long time but have been rewritten and edited to fit together in a new town, with some new friends, for a second chance to meet readers and bring even more love stories to the Louisiana bayou!

I hope you enjoy them as much as I did when I first wrote them and loved them again going back for this reimagining.

If you're a long-time reader and are "afraid" that you might have read these books before, you can check out the original titles and more information here: https://bit.ly/BadBoys-ThenNow

WELCOME TO BAD, LOUISIANA!

These boys are only called "bad" because of their hometown…

Yeah, right.

I've been to Bad several times over the years and it always makes me smile. The town itself has an interesting history. It was originally, and very briefly, settled by a bunch of Germans. Did you know that Germans use "bad" in town names to denote a spa town? Yep, that's a thing.

So, I guess in this case, there was a small hot spring outside of town and the settlers claimed that made it a spa town in the new frontier. They named the town Bad Salzuflen and they'd hoped it would attract even more settlers. Particularly of the young and female persuasion.

But, unfortunately, the 'hot spring' was actually just a particularly marshy area (no one knows why it was so much warmer… or at least they're not saying) and then, before they could figure out what to do about that, the French showed up and ran the Germans out.

Well, after that no one could pronounce or spell Bad Salzuflen, but they didn't really want to go to the trouble of renaming the whole thing, so they just dropped the Salzuflen, painted over that part of the welcome sign, and the town decided to lean into the whole *Bad* thing. Especially in more modern times.

Seriously. The hair salon is called *Bad Hair Day?* (yes with a question mark so that when they answer the phone it's, "Bad hair day?" and you say, "Yes", and they say, "Come on down and let us fix it!" And there's so much more.

Here's a quick list:
Bad Habit—coffeeshop
Bad Brakes—auto mechanic shop
Bad Brews—bar and restaurant
The Bad Egg—diner / cafe
Bad Gas—gas station and convenience store
Bad Faith Community Church—local church
Bad Hair Day?—hair salon
The Bad Place—the physical therapy clinic
Bad Medicine—the medical clinic
Bad Memories—community center

Instead of fighting it and letting everyone else mock them, the citizens decided to have some fun with it. And hey, they sell a lot of merch (like *I got Bad Gas on my roadtrip* travel mugs and *I've been to The Bad Place and survived* t-shirts) and no one ever forgets a trip to Bad!

So come on in and have some fun! It really will be a *good* time!

THE SERIES

You can read the Bad Boys of the Bayou in any order!

The Best Bad Boy: (Jase and Priscilla)
A bad boy-good girl, small town romance

Bad Medicine: (Brooke and Nick)
A hot boss, medical, small town romance

Bad Influence: (Marc and Sabrina)
An enemies to lovers, road trip/stuck together, small town
romance

Bad Taste in Men: (Luke and Bailey)
A friends to lovers, gettin'-her-groove back, small town romance

Not Such a Bad Guy: (Regan and Christopher)
A one-night-stand, mistaken identity, small town romance

Return of the Bad Boy: (Jackson and Annabelle)
A bad boy-good girl, fake relationship, small town romance

Bad Behavior: (Carter and Lacey)
A bad boy-good girl, second chance small town romance

Got It Bad: (Nolan and Randi)
A nerd-tomboy, opposites attract, small town romance

RETURN OF THE BAD BOY

*She was a real-life fantasy—the innocent librarian type wanting to
tangle with the bad boy. And oh were they going to tangle.*

The biggest bad boy of all is back in town and he's got some
unfinished business with the class goody-two-shoes. But as
much as he'd like some revenge on the snitch who got him
kicked off the championship football team, he's ten years older
and more mature and he knows there are more important things.
Most days.

Like the opportunity to come home, atone for past sins, and
prove he's ready to give back to his hometown. And he knows
just the person to help him—the same woman who brought him
down all those years ago. As a well-respected and beloved
teacher, if Annabelle is willing to take a chance on him, everyone
will know Jackson's a new man.

But he's not the only one who's changed. Though she's just as
smart as he remembers, Annabelle is also sweet, kind, loyal—
and hiding some sexy surprises behind her flowery skirts and
her cool attitude.

Suddenly proving himself to the town might be more difficult than he'd thought. Because while Jackson may have shed most of his wild ways, turns out nothing stirs his inner bad boy quite like Annabelle.

PROLOGUE

"LET'S review the rules about fighting around here."

Jackson Brady stood, feet apart, arms crossed, channeling his inner intimidating, bring-it-on football player. It had been a while since he'd been that guy, but he hadn't forgotten how to put on the you-don't-want-to-mess-with-me look.

Ironic that you're now lecturing this kid about fighting.

He barely kept from grimacing. Ironic indeed. He'd gotten into more than his share of scuffles and he'd started far more than he should admit. He'd also finished them.

Not appropriate to be feeling proud of that at the moment, big guy.

Right. He needed to be sure the kid in front of him didn't throw any more punches around here.

"Rule number one for fighting." Jackson gave the kid a hard stare. "No fighting."

The boy just glowered at him. Smart enough not to talk back, that was something.

"Rule number two for fighting," Jackson went on. "If you fight, you face me. You don't want to face me, Lucas. I've kicked your butt every time."

"That's because you know I suck at history," Lucas muttered.

"You gotta win a round now and then to get to pick the topic. It's like you don't even care."

"I *don't* even care. Why should I care about shit that happened a million years ago?"

"See, you thinking that the Civil War was a million years ago might be the reason you're getting a D in history."

Lucas didn't think that was funny.

"Look, you pull that grade up to a C, even a C minus, and you can pick the topic for Trivia Knockdown. Until then, we're on history," Jackson said.

"I'll kick your ass at math."

Jackson laughed. "That's what you think."

"I can kick all *their* butts at math." Lucas nodded toward the twenty other boys, ranging in age from fifteen to eighteen, who were standing around the backyard picnic table, eating before getting to their work.

"Maybe." Actually it was for sure. Lucas was a math whiz. "But the Pythagorean Theorem won't get you through American History. Now why'd you swing at Ryan?"

"He's a jackass."

Jackson couldn't completely disagree. Ryan had a huge chip on his shoulder. "Not a reason to hit him, man, sorry."

Jackson knew all about letting someone else's dumb ass get him into trouble.

Lucas rolled his eyes. "Alright already."

Jackson's cell phone rang in his pocket. He ignored it. He put a hand on Lucas' shoulder. "You're better than that. Hitting is sometimes the easiest way to get your point across clearly. I get it. Sometimes it feels good too. But easy isn't always better."

Lucas sighed. "Never hit. Got it."

Jackson shook his head. "That's not what I said. I said easy isn't *always* better. Sometimes you gotta do what you gotta do. But you need to use your brain to tell you when that time is, okay? You can't let your emotions get the better of you. A man knows how to keep it in check."

Lucas nodded, though it was grudging. "Okay."

The kid was seventeen. And bright. And passionate. He reminded Jackson a lot of himself at that age. And for several years after that age. Lucas let stuff get to him and he didn't have the discipline to keep his mouth and his heart from running away with him.

He'd learn.

Jackson's phone started ringing again.

"You good?" Jackson asked.

Lucas nodded.

"I'll see you for Trivia Knockdown after chores."

Lucas' shoulders slumped and he groaned, but he turned and headed for the table of after-school food.

Jackson checked his watch. "Ten minutes! I need half of you down by the barn and half of you to head to the north pasture."

He got several thumbs up.

Finally he pulled his phone from his pocket. It was a Louisiana number. His buddy Carter had called.

Jackson pressed the button to redial as he started for the barn. It only rang once before Carter answered.

"Hey, Jackson."

"Carter, how's it going man?"

Carter was one of the few ties Jackson still had with his hometown of Bad, Louisiana.

God, he loved and hated that place. Of course plenty of people cracked jokes about the town's name, but for Jackson, Bad actually did evoke a bunch of not-good emotions.

Ten years ago, Jackson had grabbed his diploma—happy as hell to have made it that far—and high-tailed it out of town. He'd left behind his Jackson-can-do-no-wrong mother, his Jackson-is-a-total-fuck-up father, all of his friends and teammates. And he hadn't been back since.

"I have some news," Carter said.

Jackson stopped walking, straightening to his full six feet, three inches. Carter's tone indicated it wasn't good news. "What?"

"It's Coach."

The two words slammed into Jackson's chest and it took him a second to breathe.

No. There was nothing wrong with Coach. How could something be wrong with Coach? That didn't make any sense. Coach Davis Karr was huge. Tough. Honest, loyal, smart—but yeah, Jackson thought, those things didn't make a guy immortal.

"What happened?" he asked Carter flatly.

"Heart attack."

Jackson sucked in a lungful of air and blew it back out, struggling for control.

"He's okay. I mean, he will be," Carter said.

"When?"

"Three days ago."

"*Three days*? What the hell, Carter?"

"Hey," Carter said firmly. "There's a lot of shit going on here."

Jackson shoved a hand through his hair. "Right. Sorry." Carter was there, in Bad, practically part of Coach's family. Carter had become the town cop, which was hilarious to everyone who had known Carter as a teen.

Jackson was the one who'd left. Who never went back to visit. Who stayed in touch with only a handful people, including Coach, sporadically via phone call and text.

That was on him.

"What can I do?" Jackson asked. "I want to help."

"I was hoping you'd say that. I'm calling because me and some of the guys are getting together to pitch in and keep the ranch going until Coach is back to it. Was hoping maybe you could come down and help."

Coach loved that damn ranch. It wasn't huge, thank God. Coach Karr had also taught and coached at the high school, ranching on the side. But that land meant the world to him.

Jackson turned and surveyed his surroundings. His own farm. From the house sitting by the road, to all the buildings, to the acres of pastures, crop fields, gardens, and the orchard—it was all his. Every sheep, pig, cow and chicken. Every blade of grass and stalk of corn. Every building, every tool—they were all his. He'd built it up, he'd made it work.

He looked at the twenty kids grabbing up the last of the sandwiches, pulling their caps on and stuffing their hands into their work gloves. They were all his too. Not really *his*, but they were a part of his very successful program to put at-risk teens to work on the farm and keep them out of trouble while teaching them about hard work, trust, teamwork and taking pride in the things they did.

This was Coach. Everything Jackson could see from where he was standing, everything he owned, everything he was proud of was because of Davis Karr. And the fact that Coach had never written him off, never turned his back... never let Jackson completely turn *his* back.

"I can be there in two days," Jackson told Carter.

"Thanks." Carter sounded relieved. "I'll tell him."

"Tell him I'll bring the cookies. I assume Elyse's hidden all of his."

Carter laughed. "She sure has."

Elyse was Coach's headstrong, sassy daughter. She was like a sister to all the guys on the football team from Jackson's era. She'd hung out with a bunch of sweaty, dirty, sometimes even bloody guys who liked to suit up and hit each other as hard as they could without blinking an eye. She'd listened to them swear and razz each other and talk about body parts and bodily functions without a single blush. She'd never let her dad's booming voice or intimidating glares get to her.

She'd also stuck around Bad and now owned the coffee shop and bakery called Bad Habit. All of the businesses in Bad leaned into the name and had tongue-in-cheek names like his buddy Marc's bar, Bad Brews. Another friend and teammate, Luke, owned Bad Brakes, the auto shop. Jase, one of his best friends from high school, had recently moved back, renovated the old strip joint his grandfather had owned and turned it into Bad Memories, the local community center, where people from Bad were going to be making lots of new memories.

The town thought it was all hilarious. Jackson thought 'hilarious' was pushing it, but it definitely made the town hard to forget.

"I'll get there as soon as I can," Jackson promised.

"See you soon."

Jackson blew out a breath as he disconnected with Carter.

He had a few things to arrange of course, but this was, after all, a self-sustaining farm. He looked at his right-hand man and friend, Cooper. He was going over work assignments with the kids, but he was making them laugh and he'd be right there to supervise and help as needed. Jackson was going to have to hope that the whole program was self-sustaining for a while.

Jackson was being *asked* to return to Bad.

He never thought he'd see that day.

CHAPTER
ONE

JACKSON BRADY LIKED WOMEN. All women. All ages, shapes, and sizes. Especially the ones who loved their curves, who were comfortable in their own skin, who celebrated their sexuality. Women were wonderful. They were soft and smelled good and generally really liked him a lot as well.

Except for one very specific exception.

And she was the person who was going to decide his fate.

Again.

Son of a bitch.

His morning meeting, the first step to becoming the new counselor for Bad High School, was with Annabelle Hartington.

Of course it was.

His buddies were probably laughing their asses off right now. Particularly Carter and Jase, the bastards. They could have at least warned him.

Jackson had arrived in Bad three days ago and during only their second private conversation, Coach had mentioned that the school was seeking a new guidance counselor. Jackson had been working with the high schools in Omaha counseling kids that were high risk for dropping out, gang activity, drugs, crime, suicide and more. Each school had their own guidance counselor but Jackson stepped in for the entire district for the really challenging cases.

He was more than qualified to counsel the kids in Bad and it had only taken him ten minutes with Coach to realize that he was home to stay. This was his chance to be the person Coach had always believed he could be.

But first he had to get through Annabelle.

Jackson scanned her from head to toe. He hadn't seen her in ten years and she had *not* looked like this in high school. He liked women in three things—tight jeans, short skirts, or nothing at all. Not necessarily in that order.

None of those applied to the woman in front of him at the moment. Annabelle wore a flowing skirt that reached to her ankles, a loose blousy thing on top and a frown.

The skirt covered everything up but it was pretty and girly—two things he'd never associated with Annabelle before. Her hair was down and he honestly couldn't remember ever seeing her hair in anything but braids or a ponytail. And he'd known this girl since kindergarten.

Her hair hung nearly to the curve of her lower back in gentle waves that looked soft and feminine. For just a flash, Jackson wondered how her hair smelled. Like flowers, he'd bet. Or maybe strawberries.

He shook that off quickly. If he got close enough to smell Annabelle's hair, she'd likely knee him in the balls.

He chalked up the crazy thought of smelling her to being a guy. He knew he had testosterone to spare and it often affected him in unfortunate ways—usually making him run his mouth, fight, drink, swear and screw.

He was proud of the fact that he had much more control now as a twenty-eight-year-old man than he had when he'd last seen Annabelle at age eighteen, but that didn't mean he didn't still have urges.

Speaking of urges—Jackson leaned in, staring at Annabelle's mouth. This girl hadn't worn lip gloss one single day when he'd known her but now her lips were shiny and peach-colored.

Maybe she smelled, and tasted, like peaches.

The frown, however, was quite familiar.

"Mr. Brady," she said coolly.

He grinned. No one called him Mr. Brady. That was hilarious. "Hey, Annabelle."

She straightened. "I go by AJ now."

Jackson pulled the chair in front of her desk around and straddled it, leaning on the back. "What's the J stand for?"

Her eyes narrowed.

"Come on. That won't be hard to find out if you don't tell me." His own mother probably knew.

"Why do you care?"

He wasn't sure that he did. He did know that his asking made her bristle and that was fun for him for some reason.

Actually, he knew the reason. This woman had caused him a lot of trouble. Causing her a little discomfort seemed like his due.

He shrugged. "I'm not asking for the key to your diary. Why do you not want me to know?"

Was needling her immature? Of course. Was he above teasing a girl from his past just to piss her off? He hoped so. But he was still doing it.

She sighed. "Josephine. If you must know."

"Annabelle Josephine," he said thoughtfully. "I like it." She looked much softer and more feminine than she ever had in high school. He remembered her in jeans, loose plaid shirts over t-shirts, Converse tennis shoes and ponytails. The flowy skirt was nice. Her hair down was beautiful. And he'd bet damn good money she smelled delicious. All over. Yet AJ seemed so much more formal than Annabelle.

"You can call me Ms. Hartington."

He gave her another grin. "I don't think so."

She raised an eyebrow. "Excuse me?"

"I've known you since we were five, Annabelle. I'm not one of your students and, frankly, I'm not really into a lot of formality."

"You don't say." She pulled her chair out and took a seat behind her desk, prim and proper as all get out.

Jackson slumped farther and wished he had a cap on so he could turn it around, brim in back, and look *really* unconcerned. But no, he'd dressed up. He was in a button-down shirt and pants that weren't denim. He definitely cared about this interview. But something about Annabelle made him not want to let on.

Immature for sure.

And stupid. He wanted this job and she was the first person he had to impress—or at least get through—to get it.

Annabelle might be the head of the search committee for a new guidance counselor for Bad High, but he was a hell of a counselor, and he had the track record and recommendations to prove it. His approach worked and he wasn't going to change it to impress Miss Hoity-Toity.

She was in charge of this first interview. That was all fine and good. Someone had to vet candidates to avoid taking up the time of the whole committee and school board with people who wouldn't be a good fit. Annabelle knew the town of Bad and Bad High as well as anyone. She'd grown up here, attended K through twelve here, had been teaching here since college graduation.

Plus she was judgmental as hell and loved to share her opinion. She'd very likely volunteered to head the committee.

But her past opinions of him better not play into this. He was a good counselor. And he wanted this job more than anyone else they would see. He was a hometown boy too. For better or worse, that meant he knew this town and school—and they all knew him.

Tension knotted his shoulders and upper back and he rolled his neck, willing himself to calm down. He was jumping ahead.

Yes, he and Annabelle had a history. An unpleasant one at that. And like any good small town, everyone in Bad knew their history, knew his past transgressions, knew that his wild streak hadn't ended with high school graduation. But people changed. He believed that, knew it was possible, believed it about himself. He was set on proving it to the town. So he had to give her the benefit of the doubt here.

And maybe stop trying to piss her off on purpose.

Jackson took a deep breath, then blew it out. "Thank you for taking the time to see me."

She raised an eyebrow, but opened the folder in front of her without a word. He recognized his resume on the top. She scanned over it, tapping her pen against the desk as she read.

As if she hadn't already read it. He was sure she'd studied it. Annabelle Hartington had always been the most organized, most prepared student in their class. That kind of stuff didn't change and there was no way she didn't know his resume and application by heart.

He needed to sit quietly and not antagonize her further before she started the interview.

But for some damn reason he said, "Kind of ironic that we're meeting in this room, isn't it?"

Annabelle's head came up quickly and she stared at him with her mouth open.

Yeah, he couldn't believe he'd said it either.

Well, he could of course. That was exactly the stupid-ass shit he'd always done. Exactly the kind of thing he'd worked hard to overcome.

After a moment, she shut her mouth and leaned on the pages in front of her and removed her glasses to look him directly in the eye. "Should we get that elephant out of the room?"

Was there something bigger than an elephant they could compare the subject to? Because an elephant didn't seem imposing enough. Maybe a T-Rex?

"Maybe we should." He tried to sound nonchalant.

"Then let's put it out there. I once walked in on you and our student teacher having sex in this very room. I told the principal, you got suspended, she got fired and you didn't play in the state championship football game. The biggest game of the season."

Jackson swallowed hard and tried not to show that he was swallowing hard.

Damn. That was a pretty good recap.

She hadn't included how the whole situation had torn out his heart, spiraled him out of control, caused an irreparable rift between him and his father, embarrassed his mother and strained pretty much every friendship he had.

But otherwise she'd summarized it nicely.

"That's about how I remember it," he commented easily. As if it hadn't been the most pivotal moment of his life.

"And you're still angry with me about it." Annabelle was watching him carefully.

He opened his mouth to deny it. Being angry about it ten years later would mean that he could really hold a grudge; that he hadn't moved on, hadn't grown as much as he kept telling himself he had.

But yeah, dammit, he was still angry about it.

He leaned closer to her desk, tipping his chair onto two legs. "Tell me why you did it. That's what I've never understood. Everything would have been fine if you'd just kept quiet. We weren't hurting anyone."

Annabelle pressed her lips together, seemingly thinking about his request.

It was true that he'd been a student having sex in the school with a student teacher—someone in an authority position. But he'd been eighteen, Jenny Schneider had been twenty-one and they'd both been willing participants. The school, and his mother, seemed to believe that he'd been taken advantage of, but the truth was that he'd started the flirtation and had absolutely wanted to have sex with the hot young teacher. He'd been a horny eighteen-year-old kid. Her short skirts and red curls had gotten to him, what could he say?

Annabelle had caught them the third time they'd had sex. First time in the school, but still, it wasn't as if it had been one sudden, spontaneous what-the-hell moment. They'd had a relationship. At least, Jackson had thought they had.

Jenny had dropped him fast enough after everything blew up.

Of course, the threat of legal action hadn't helped. Jackson hadn't been a minor, but his father was an imposing son of a bitch and he'd given Jenny all kinds of bullshit threats. Credible or not, Jackson had, apparently, not been worth the hassle.

"I was concerned about you," Annabelle finally said.

He felt his eyes widen and the chair legs hit the floor. "Concerned about me?"

"She was older. She was a teacher."

"A student teacher."

"She still shouldn't have been messing around with a student." Annabelle frowned.

"So it wasn't concern for me so much as disapproval of her not following the rules."

"She was exploiting you."

He laughed. "Honey, I never once felt exploited. I was having a hell of a good time."

Annabelle was unfazed. "It was wrong. You were a kid. She was a teacher."

"I was eighteen, Annabelle. She was twenty-one. Three years. And I was willing. There was nothing to be worried about." He'd been crazy about Jenny. She'd been a nice girl, sweet, quiet, almost shy. In spite of being three years older than him, she'd seemed younger. He'd been able to make her blush so easily. He'd been drawn to her from day one.

Annabelle chewed on the inside of her cheek for a moment, as if trying to decide something. Then she took a deep breath, licked her lips and said, "You were falling for her."

That took him aback. "What?"

Annabelle nodded. "You were. I could tell."

Jackson didn't know what to say to that. He *had* been falling for her. He'd fallen fast and hard. He was suddenly very interested in what Annabelle Hartington knew and how she knew it.

"You were worried because you thought I was falling for her, so when you walked in on us, you decided to save me by turning us in and ruining my life?"

She grimaced a little at the end, but nodded. "I might have overreacted in my desire to protect you."

Jackson had about a million thoughts rolling around in his head. Annabelle had noticed something more intimate than him sitting in the chair behind the desk with Jenny on his lap, riding him like a cowgirl. Annabelle had noticed that he'd been falling for Jenny.

How the hell had she known that? And why did she care?

"So are you apologizing to me?" he asked, unable to come up with anything else.

Annabelle met his eyes again. "No."

"No? You admitted you overreacted."

"I did. But I'm not sorry."

"You're not?" Jackson frowned at her. "You fucked everything up for me."

She didn't look impressed by his scowl or his language. "*You* fucked everything up for yourself, Mr. Brady."

Jackson stared at her, torn between laughing and yelling. Annabelle Hartington had just said the word "fucked" to him. And she was calling him Mr. Brady again. And she was…right.

He knew that. He had taken responsibility for what had happened. It had taken him a few years and a couple of psych classes in college and more than a couple of conversations with Coach, but he had finally realized that he'd been in control of his actions and needed to accept that the consequences of those actions were on him.

The thought of Coach made Jackson's heart clench and he

focused on the desktop and waited for the pain/panic to pass. Coach was going to be okay. He was. But Jackson still couldn't shake the feeling of dread thinking about a world without Coach. Jackson would be…hell, he didn't even know—an alcoholic? In jail without Coach? And now Coach needed Jackson and Jackson was, by God, going to be there. In fact, Jackson was going to be there for good now. He had to get this damned job.

But when he looked back up at Annabelle, he saw something in her eyes that made him stupid again. Because she did look a little guilty.

When he was stupid, he got mouthy and said stuff he'd later regret.

"You must have been paying pretty close attention to me," he commented. Stupidly. "I mean, for you to notice how I felt about her. How did you figure that out?"

If Annabelle had gotten prissy and told him to shut up and focus on the interview, he would have. But instead she blushed.

Beer and tequila made him reckless, sports talk made him cocky, Friday nights in the fall on a football field gave him a rush that made him feel invincible. But nothing made him feel like a big-shot and act like an idiot like a pretty girl blushing for him.

"Annabelle," he asked, using the soft drawl that his Louisiana upbringing had given him and about sixteen years of flirting had perfected. "How did you know that I was falling for Jenny?"

She swallowed, and for the first time since he'd stepped into the room, she didn't meet his eyes when she spoke. "I…knew you."

His eyebrows definitely rose at that. "Excuse me?" He and Annabelle Hartington had spent maybe a total of five minutes alone together ever. And that five minutes had been in increments of a few seconds at a time over the years. They had not been friends. They knew each other only as two people who had been in school together for thirteen years. They'd had no friends, no activities, no interests in common.

"I paid attention." She did look up then. "It's amazing what you can pick up and figure out when you're the quiet odd man out. People often forgot I was there, or didn't think I was paying attention. It's interesting what people will say and do when they don't think anyone is listening or watching."

Annabelle had waitressed at The Bad Egg, the downtown diner, in high school. It was one of those details he'd known about her in the back of his mind but hadn't really realized he knew. Like that she'd never worn skirts or lip gloss in high school.

She *had* been the quiet odd man out. No question. She'd been incredibly studious, serious about everything, always with her nose in a book. Even as a little kid, she didn't play tag or jump rope or swing with the other girls. She would sit at the top of the jungle gym and read. She would finish her work first and then ask for extra credit. She was the only one in class who was happy when it was too cold or rainy to go outside for recess or PE class.

In high school, she'd always put off this I'm-not-interested vibe. She didn't date. She hadn't gone to one single dance or party all through high school. Not homecoming, not prom, not one beer party at the river.

She'd also been the teacher's pet, and by far the girl you wanted to be assigned as your lab partner or to be put in your group for the projects in English or Social Studies classes.

Of course, the one time she'd been matched as Jackson's lab partner in Chemistry, she'd gone to the teacher immediately after class and the next day, they'd already been reassigned.

"So what did I do or say that made you figure out how I felt about Jenny?" He really wanted to know this. It was interesting —and maybe a little creepy—to think she'd been paying attention to him and he'd had no clue.

"I observed how you treated all the different girls who were always around. There were the ones you liked and you flirted with, there were the ones who liked you and you tolerated as adoring fans, there were the two you couldn't stand—Brittni and Amanda—and then there were the ones you were crazy about—Hope and Jenny. Miss Schneider."

Jackson was having a hard time taking a deep breath. A lot of people knew he couldn't stand Brittni and Amanda. Brittni had dated and cheated on one of Jackson's best friends. Amanda was a bitch. He was hardly the only one who felt that way about her. And everyone knew that he and Hope had been in love. She'd been his girlfriend sophomore year until her family had moved to Tennessee. They'd been as serious as two sixteen-year-olds could be. But that Annabelle had noticed, *watched*, how he treated all the various girls was...weird.

"You were stalking me?"

She laughed. He hadn't been expecting that. He looked at her with surprise. He also noted that she had a very nice laugh and that she was very pretty when she smiled.

"'No, I wasn't stalking you. I was trying to learn."

"Learn?"

She nodded. "Social interactions have always fascinated me because they've always been uncomfortable for me. I hate parties, I hate thinking about what to wear for a certain occasion, hate trying to read body language and decipher tone of voice and facial expressions. I like things straightforward and simple. But that's not how the world works, so I watched all of the guys and girls interact and took note of what they did and how it was received and the results of those interactions."

She stopped talking and her eyes widened as if she couldn't believe she'd said all of that.

Jackson was pretty floored as well.

"It was one big social experiment," Jackson commented.

He'd had no idea she'd been watching him. And everyone else. He was sure no one in their class realized everything Annabelle had probably picked up about each of them.

"Not an experiment," she said, a bit meekly now. "I didn't do anything to influence the interactions or to prove or disprove any theories. I just observed."

"Wow. Creepy."

She bit her lip again and nodded. "It does sound that way when I say it out loud."

He laughed at that, surprised that she could be self-deprecating and that she amused him.

"You have me all figured out then?" he asked.

She hesitated. He cocked an eyebrow. Finally she nodded. "At least at age eighteen, I knew you pretty well. And I knew you were falling for Jenny."

Jackson sat back and regarded Annabelle. How had they gotten here? This topic was pretty crazy and way off from how he'd expected this conversation to go.

"Do you know enough about me to recommend me for the guidance counselor position?"

Seemingly jarred back to the actual reason for their meeting, Annabelle straightened and again opened his folder. "I can see potential. You were, after all, in the guidance counselor's office— and other offices—a lot during high school."

Again, he chuckled. That was exactly the reason he'd been drawn to being a school counselor. He knew where the troubled kids were coming from and could relate a lot of his own stories to win them over and gain their trust. He also knew that bullshit got him exactly nowhere. He was a straight shooter. Like Annabelle claimed to be.

"I've had a lot of success with kids both as a school counselor and with my farm."

She nodded. "Tell me more about that."

It was all there in front of her, but Jackson had no trouble talking about his pet project.

He leaned into the back of the chair again. "Some things that helped me out a lot when I was off track were Coach, hard work on the ranch and my friends. Whenever I was having trouble, Coach would give me advice and then send me out to work.

Working alone with hard manual labor, just the sun and the fields and animals, had a way of clearing my head. I'd think about what he'd told me and I'd let it sink in. Once I left Bad, I didn't have that anymore. And I got off track again."

Annabelle was studying him and listening raptly. He wondered if this was left over from her high school days of being the observer, or if she truly was that interested. "I see you have some things on your record that might be of concern."

"Those were before I finished my degree. Since I've been teaching—including student teaching," he added with a small smile that she, surprisingly, returned, "I haven't had any run-ins with the law."

"Arrested for drunk and disorderly twice, two minor in possession charges, assault." She looked up at him. "Assault?"

"Guy in a bar bothering a girl who didn't want to be bothered," Jackson said calmly. He wasn't embarrassed by that charge. He'd do that again in a heartbeat.

"You weren't the guy bothering the girl, were you?" Annabelle asked, but she did it with a little sparkle in her eye.

Was Annabelle Hartington teasing him?

Jackson leaned in, wanting a closer look at her eyes. "I don't bother women."

Her cheeks got a little pink.

Nice.

He grinned. "I'll admit in my younger days, I sometimes mouthed off or swung before I thought better of it. I drank and partied and basically tried to forget about how messed up my life had become. And then, thank God, Coach finally made me pull my head out of my ass, I straightened up and I've been good ever since."

Annabelle opened her mouth with a reply, but quickly snapped it shut again, chewing on her lip.

Oh, he had to hear this. "What were you about to say?"

"Nothing." She focused on the folder again. "I would agree that these past issues shouldn't have a bearing now. In fact, a case could be made that they also help you relate to students who are having a hard time."

He nodded. He appreciated that. "What were you about to say?"

She looked up. "Nothing I *should* say."

He gave her a half grin. "I know from experience that it can be liberating to say things you shouldn't once in a while."

She seemed intrigued by that. "I was going to say that just because you haven't had any further legal issues, doesn't mean you know how to be good."

He stared at her a moment. Then he laughed. Out loud. She did know a few things about him. "How do you think I've been bad?" he asked, grinning.

She blushed again.

Yeah, he'd been bad that way.

He laughed again. "I actually try to be really *good*, Annabelle."

The blush deepened and he knew she'd caught his meaning. "Wow, you just can't help it, can you?"

"Help what?"

"Flirting with anyone who has breasts."

Of course, his gaze dropped to her breasts when she said that. He was a guy, and a pretty simple one at that. Mention breasts and he looked for the closest pair.

The ones in front of him now were not bad. From what he could tell. He did prefer fitted shirts to the loose type that Annabelle was wearing though.

"It kind of seems like maybe you're flirting a little too."

She shook her head. "Accident."

He laughed at that too. "Accidental or not, you're doing it."

"Are we talking just sex here or are you good at drinking, fighting, and partying and not getting caught too?"

He had no idea if this was helping or hurting his interview, but he was suddenly having a good time. He'd been born a flirt and it was hard to suppress the compulsion a lot of the time. He would have thought Annabelle might be the one woman who didn't bring that out in him but...apparently not. And she didn't blush and get flustered or seductive. She blushed and then called him on it.

There was something there that made him want to go further. He wasn't even sure she knew she was blushing. Things could have obviously changed a lot in ten years, but Annabelle didn't have flirting experience from high school, that was for sure.

"I try to be good at everything I do," he said. "Yes, I still party some, but I drink in moderation, I don't fight and I try to stay out of jail."

"Probably a good thing, considering what you want to do for a living."

He agreed. "I've been a school counselor for the past five years. I've been running the program at the farm for the past three. We bring kids in who either need somewhere to go besides home, or who have been through the system and are having trouble with staying clean during probation. It's a fully functioning, self-sufficient farm. The kids do the farm work, help keep the house up, and then get to enjoy the products of their work—the food and a share in the money from livestock and hay sales. They learn to fix everything from roofs to fences to motors. They learn how to build things. They learn how to cook, clean, do laundry. They learn to budget money, manage their time, work with different personalities. They get to stay at the house whenever they want or need to. But they have to get along, pull their share of the weight, and keep their grades up. We also have fun —horseback riding, hayrack rides, bonfires, campouts, fishing and hunting."

Annabelle was staring at him.

Jackson shifted on his chair. He'd gone off about the farm. He often did that. He loved that place, was prouder of it than any football accomplishment he'd ever had.

"You live at the farm?"

"Yes. I own the land, the house, the livestock...everything."

"Do you have help?"

"Volunteers."

"How do you deal with behavior problems?"

"We have a system. We have house meetings. I rely on peer pressure a lot. Everyone has a role and if they don't do their part, the system falls down. The kids who want to be there and care, keep the ones with bad attitudes on track. Or they leave. I'm not a state- or city-funded program. I don't have to keep anyone there who doesn't want it or deserve it. I give second and third and fourth chances, but they have to show me they want it. And we have group and individual counseling sessions that they have to attend."

"Do you get grant money?"

"A little. But the farm is able to supply most of what we need. We take on projects for others too—home or farm building repair, small engine repair, clean-up projects—for pay. We get some donations. But mostly we produce the things we need."

"But you use your own money sometimes to keep it going," Annabelle said.

He shrugged again. "Sometimes."

She sat looking at him for several seconds. Finally she seemed to shake herself out of whatever that was and sat back. She closed the folder. "I've read and heard what I needed to for now. I think this could be a good fit. But I'm not the only one you have to convince."

"I know that." Jackson caught and held her gaze. "But you're a big part. Everyone knows and respects you. And they know our history. If you give your thumbs up, that will matter. People will listen to you."

She licked her lips. "I know. Especially with…everything that happened before. So you also understand that I have to know my recommendation won't come back and bite me in the butt."

And of course he couldn't help but think that he might like to *see* her butt. That damn flowy skirt wouldn't allow that though.

He reined in his thoughts. He needed to behave. Even more

than usual. Running the farm, being his own boss, was liberating. He could swear when he needed to, say stupid shit, do stupid shit. He wasn't going to get fired. But what made *him* behave was being a role model to all the kids who came to the farm. He took that seriously. He knew how much having a strong, positive role model could mean in someone's life.

Annabelle got up and came around her desk, taking a seat at one of the students' desks beside him. She crossed her legs and his gaze dropped to her feet.

He did a double take and then flat-out stared. She wore tiny strappy sandals that showed off bright-blue toenail polish, a toe ring on the right foot, and a tiny tattoo just below her left big toe. Of a...symbol. It reminded him of something musical but he couldn't remember what it was called.

Annabelle didn't seem like the type to have a random tattoo picked out of a catalog at the last minute. It had to mean something. He suddenly wanted to know what.

But his curiosity didn't take away from the fact the tattoo was unexpectedly sexy.

The ink, toe ring and polish also told him something very important—Annabelle Hartington was not the girl he remembered.

"What are you going to do about the farm and everything if you get this job, Jackson?"

He looked up at her. She'd called him Jackson, rather than Mr. Brady. Did that mean something? Why did he think it did? Why did he care?

"I'll maintain ownership and oversee the program, but I have a buddy who's going to take it over. He's been there working with us, helping out for about a year. I'd like to do something similar here. I'm going to look into some land in the area."

She seemed pleased with that answer. "It's an impressive program. I Googled you before we met today."

That didn't surprise him a bit. He'd known she was perfectly prepared. "Thanks. I appreciate you being that interested."

"My interest is in the well-being of the students in Bad."

"I know."

"But I think I can honestly say that you passed the initial interview."

He grinned widely, relief sweeping through him. "Yeah?"

"Yeah," she answered with a smile.

Thank God. Step one down. Likely the hardest step. If he could win Annabelle over, he could win anyone else over.

"How's Coach?"

Jackson found that his eyes had drifted to her feet again. The blue polish seemed out of place but it was the toe ring and tattoo that really threw him. He wondered if she had any other tattoos. What would they be of? Butterflies and flowers, if he had to guess. And they'd be small. But where would she put them?

"Jackson, are you okay?"

He looked from the tattoo to her face again. Was he okay? He was feeling a little...flummoxed, actually. And she might be impressed with his use of that big word.

"Yep. I'm good. Great. I'm very happy the interview has gone well."

"How's Coach?"

She'd asked about Coach before too. Damn. How had he gotten distracted from *that*? That she asked made him feel warmer toward her. Coach was like a father to Jackson. Better than his own father for sure. Jackson owed him everything.

"Coach is better. Getting stronger but not—" Jackson's voice caught and he cleared his throat. "Not himself yet."

Jackson knew he wasn't the only one of the guys who had been struck by how weak Coach was. When they'd played for him, he'd been a big, solid guy who could move the tackling dummies as far as any of the linemen. He had a big voice that could be heard from one end zone to the other, a big sense of humor and an even bigger heart. He'd be the first to kick your ass if you were messing up but he'd also be the first to tell you he was proud of you if you did something right.

There was something about him that made all of the guys who played for him want to do right all the time.

"I think it's great how you're all coming back to help him out," Annabelle said.

Jackson nodded. It had been a no-brainer for him, but he'd been pleased to find all of the other guys were doing the same and rallying around. "It's good to be a team again." He'd missed it more than he'd realized. He'd let his teammates down by getting suspended for their championship run and he'd felt distant from the guys ever since. Except for Carter and Jase. Jase had left Bad right after graduation as well, but Jackson knew Jase had always been just a phone call away. Even when he didn't deserve it.

Annabelle did that thing again where she simply sat looking at him and Jackson wondered what she was thinking. Or seeing. She'd been more observant than he'd realized in high school. Who knew what she was realizing about him now?

"I'll pass on my recommendation for you to meet with the entire committee." She stood quickly and went back behind her desk.

So they were done.

Jackson stretched to his feet and turned the chair back to face her desk. "Thanks for your time, Annabelle."

"It was...nice talking to you, Jackson." She almost seemed surprised.

He grinned. "Ditto."

It had been. Strangely.

"I'll let you know when the committee plans to meet."

"You can find me at Coach's or you have my cell number."

She nodded. "I'll talk to you soon."

"I'll be waiting for your call."

CHAPTER
TWO

JACKSON BRADY HAD CHANGED.

A lot.

Annabelle couldn't shake that thought for two days. Even as she stood in line for her morning coffee and muffin at Bad Habit, the downtown coffeehouse, she was thinking about it.

She'd been dreading that meeting. Jackson had been intimidating in high school with his devil-may-care attitude and his constant risk taking. He'd also been intimidatingly popular, always surrounded by people, and intimidatingly good-looking.

And yes, Annabelle had always found incredibly outgoing, popular, beautiful people a bit intimidating.

She simply didn't know what to say to them. She had no idea what made them tick, why they did the things they did, why they wanted or needed all that adoration and stimulation. Which was why she'd started studying them. She hadn't done it on purpose—at first. She hadn't skulked in the shadows or eavesdropped intentionally. She'd just started paying attention, trying to figure it all out.

And she'd come up with some interesting realizations and theories. But she wasn't convinced that she truly *understood* any of it.

Give her pajamas, popcorn and her couch on a Friday night, alone or not, over a ballgame, concert, show or party. Give her a book and a comfy chair over a girls' night margarita fest at the bar. Give her a piano and some new sheet music over a backyard barbecue or pool party.

She loved being alone. She was good at it.

But she was a minority, she knew.

The coffee shop was loud this morning. She was fifth in line and felt surrounded by the conversations and laughter.

She moved up to fourth in line and thought about her to-do list for the day and—as had been happening since their meeting two days before—Jackson. He really had changed a lot.

Except for the fact that he was still intimidatingly good-looking. She'd been alright during their meeting because she'd had the upper hand. He needed her approval. And they'd been on her turf.

Of course, that had all shifted when he'd pointed out the fact that it was the same room where she'd caught him with Miss Schneider ten years before. Not that Annabelle hadn't realized that. She'd just been staunchly ignoring it.

It was her classroom now. She ruled that room. The people who walked into that room wanted to impress her. Needed to, even. She wasn't mean or overly strict, but she was well-known as the toughest teacher in the school. She had high standards for her students and she believed in challenging them. And still her students liked her. She got e-mails all the time from past students thanking her and she'd been mentioned in four valedictory addresses.

She was in charge in that room. So she didn't think about it being where Jackson had been doing Miss Schneider. Until he'd brought it up. And every damn detail of that day had come rushing back.

She moved up to third in line and tried to concentrate on the next song playing from the overhead speakers instead of replaying that day in October ten years ago.

But no. There was no blocking that memory now that it had started.

She'd gone looking for Mrs. Wilson, the English teacher, to ask about the paper that was due the next week. It had been after hours, but Annabelle had been practicing piano in the music room and had lost track of time. She'd known it was unlikely anyone was left in the school, but she'd thought she'd try swinging by the room just in case.

The door had been closed but not latched and she'd heard noises from the room. Assuming Mrs. Wilson was in there, Annabelle had knocked and pushed the door open.

And froze in her tracks.

She'd wanted to look away, she really had. She'd wanted to run. She'd wanted to sneak out and pretend she hadn't seen anything at all. But her feet wouldn't move, her eyes wouldn't blink and she'd heard the *oh my God* come out of her mouth without any conscious effort at all.

Jackson had been sitting in the chair behind the desk with Miss Schneider straddling his lap, her shirt and bra pulled up, exposing her breasts. One breast had been covered with one of his hands, the other by his mouth. She'd said "oh my God" right before Annabelle had. Though Miss Schneider had moaned the words and Annabelle had more or less shrieked them.

Annabelle remembered everything after that happening as if in slow motion. They'd both turned their heads toward her, Annabelle had felt a rush of heat and then cold, Miss Schneider had almost fallen off Jackson's lap, Jackson had fumbled with his jeans that were only unzipped and spread open.

Annabelle remembered feeling tears rush up and sting her eyes, remembered being frustrated and confused by that, and then spinning from the door, tripping over her own feet, and running for the front of the school.

Jackson had run after her. She could recall the sound of his feet pounding down the hallway behind her. She'd never been an athlete and he was the star running back on the football team, bound for a state championship, but she outran him that day. And managed to wedge herself in between the building and the driver's ed car right before he thundered past.

She could practically feel her heart hammering in her chest now like she had that day.

She'd stayed in that protected space for almost half an hour. Her head had been spinning. She'd been shocked and confused and angry.

It certainly had nothing to do with any kind of relationship with Jackson. It had been about her admiration for Miss Schneider. Annabelle had always held teachers to a higher standard. She believed they went into education to help kids and make an impact on the future. Cheesy, but true. And then…that.

She also remembered feeling worried about Jackson. Maybe not because of what had been going on in the classroom specifically. He'd seemed to be enjoying himself there. But she'd already noticed that he had feelings for their young teacher and she knew what kind of trouble they could get into for what they'd been doing.

Annabelle moved ahead in line again and the song ended. There was a beat of silence and in that moment she heard low male laughter behind her. Normally she would have ignored it or tuned it out, but for some reason this laugh made her turn.

Sure enough, it was Jackson.

He was talking with three men from Autre, the town just down the bayou. The town that was *supposed* to be Bad's biggest rival. Except that Zander Landry, their cop, and Knox, their city manager, came to Bad Habit *all the time*.

And then there was Michael LeClaire. Autre's very hot, very heroic, fire chief and lead EMT. Everyone in the entire parish liked Michael, even if he was from Autre. Apparently, even people who had been away from Bad for ten years.

There were two people between her and them and Annabelle did an abrupt about-face and took a deep breath.

Maybe Jackson wouldn't notice her or, at least, wouldn't talk to her. She wasn't great before she'd had her coffee and with the vivid memories of him doing Miss Schneider—or had she been doing him?—fresh in her mind, Annabelle wasn't sure she could look at him and make small talk. She could still remember the glimpse of his erection she'd gotten before he'd covered it with denim and vaulted out of the chair. She'd been remembering that glimpse on and off for ten years.

And she'd never been great at small talk with Michael. Unlike the men in Bad she'd known all her life, Michael was an unknown entity. She wasn't sure what to talk to him about. She didn't know much about fires and she thought it might come off rude to ask if he knew anything about American or English Literature.

All she really knew about him was that he was incredibly handsome with his medium brown skin, dark brown eyes, quick smile, and that uniform and badge he wore. He positively *exuded* confidence and an air of command while also being friendly and charming every single time she'd been around him.

Bad had their own fire department, but the two towns often did trainings together and helped one another on big scenes. Michael had also agreed to come talk to the kids at the elementary school when some of the teachers had petitioned to have him lead the assembly instead of the firefighters from Bad.

The youngest member of the Bad department was fifty and the teachers had claimed a younger firefighter would be more relatable and inspirational to the kids. Not surprisingly, all of those teachers were women. As was the principal who had agreed. Annabelle had heard the talk in the teacher's break room. She knew very well why they'd asked the charming, muscular fire chief from the next town to make the twenty-minute drive.

And that day, watching him with those little kids, she'd started crushing on single dad and heroic good guy, Michael LeClaire. Just like every other single woman in the parish.

Fortunately, Michael seemed to enjoy hanging out at Bad

Brews, the bar in town where a lot of Annabelle's friends and classmates spent time. So she ran into him from time to time and…watched him interact with everyone else. Sure, she should probably *talk* to him more often. But watching him was no hardship.

Annabelle fanned her face. Was it warm in here? Maybe she should get an iced coffee today.

She looked around the shop as the man in front of her finally finished placing his order. How were all the other women in the place carrying on as if everything was normal and there wasn't testosterone permeating the very air they breathed?

Her gaze landed on one of the young baristas. The girl was stirring a spoon around in a cup. And stirring. And stirring. Her attention was glued to Jackson and the Autre men.

Maybe not *every* woman in the place was carrying on normally. That made Annabelle feel a little better.

Annabelle had a thing for Michael, plain and simple, and she had no idea what to do about it. So she was doing nothing about it. Which was resulting in, as would be expected, nothing happening between them.

"Skinny caramel latte and a lemon poppy seed muffin," she told the girl behind the counter.

"Regular or sugar-free?"

"Regular."

The girl punched the keys on the register. "Nine seventeen."

"I've got it."

A deep voice and warm body were suddenly beside her, right up against her as a matter of fact, and Annabelle looked up to see Jackson smiling down at her.

"Mornin'," he greeted.

Damn, that smile. She was aware that she hadn't seen that thing directed at her at all until two days ago. It was powerful. She was grateful that up until October of their senior year, he hadn't noticed her enough to smile at her, and after that day in the English classroom, he'd only had scowls for her.

He placed an order as well and handed the cashier money, then he nudged Annabelle toward the pick-up area. "How are you this morning?"

As his mouth moved, she tried very hard not to think about how his lips had looked on Jenny Schneider's nipple.

How was it possible that she'd catalogued so many details in the ten seconds she'd stood rooted in that doorway?

"Are you hot?"

She blinked at him. "Huh?"

"Are you hot? Sick? You look flushed."

Horny, as a matter of fact. But there was no way in *hell* she was going to say that to him.

"I'm good." The barista called out her order and she spun away from him, thankful for the distraction. "Thanks for breakfast," she said. "You didn't have to do that."

"I was hoping to run into you." He stepped in front of her when she tried to move past him with her muffin and coffee.

"You were?" She hadn't called him yet about the committee meeting because a meeting time hadn't been determined. "I don't have any details for you yet, I'm sorry."

"Not that."

He reached past her for his coffee and his arm brushed her shoulder. She also took a deep breath—because a girl had to breathe after all—and sucked in a nice lungful of his scent. Soap, alfalfa and laundry detergent. No cologne. That surprised her for some reason.

He leaned away, coffee retrieved, and she worked on looking unaffected.

"Hey, AJ."

Unaffected by *Jackson*. Because she was *affected* by Michael.

"Hi, Michael, how are you?"

"Great."

He gave her a grin and Annabelle waited for it to fry a couple of brain cells like Jackson's seemed to.

Nothing.

But that was *good*. She wanted to date Michael. She couldn't date a guy who struck her dumb by simply smiling at her. That would be awkward.

"Michael was just leaving," Jackson said.

"Was I?" Michael asked. "I thought you asked me to coffee."

Annabelle glanced behind Michael and saw Zander and Knox making their way up the steps to the second-floor loft.

"We just happened to run into each other outside," Jackson said. "And that was not what I asked you."

He was standing really close to her. Annabelle could see that his jaw was tense and he was clearly trying to communicate something to Michael with only a look. Something Michael was missing. Possibly on purpose.

"Am I interrupting something?" she asked.

But she hadn't interrupted. If anything, Jackson had insinuated himself into *her* morning.

Michael smirked at Jackson. "I think maybe I'm the one interrupting."

Jackson gave a little cough.

"Because you're right, what you asked me was if I'd seen Annabelle." Michael looked at Annabelle and gave her a wink. "Took me a minute to figure out who he was talking about since you're going by AJ now."

The wink was nice.

"You were looking for me?" Annabelle asked.

"Yes," Jackson said. "I wanted to see if you'd like to have dinner with me tonight. I didn't get your number the other day."

Annabelle felt her mouth drop open. "You're asking me out?"

Jackson gave her a half smile. Even a half smile made her stomach flip. Damn.

"Annabelle?"

She realized she was staring at him. "Yes?"

"What do you say? Dinner tonight?"

Sure, Jackson Brady and Annabelle Hartington were going to go to dinner together. Talk about the weirdest date in history.

He'd hated her for…well, a while. He'd seemed very matter-of-fact about everything the other day. And he did, actually, seem over it. In ten years, a mature adult with a decent amount of self-awareness would be over it, so she'd been glad to see that in him. Still, there had been a long period of time when she was sure he had a voodoo doll of her or her picture pinned to a dartboard or both.

She hadn't been hugely popular in town after all of that, either. Thank God the team had won the championship even without Jackson. But in the week leading up to the first playoff game, Annabelle had been despised by the entire football team, most of the student body, and a majority of the town.

This was Louisiana. Football was right up there with family and church as far as what mattered in life. And *winning* at football was everything. Without Jackson there had been a chance that the championship was out of reach.

But they'd won, and Jackson had, after all, been the one at fault and eventually things died down. A bit. For Annabelle anyway.

Jackson, on the other hand, had gone a little crazy. He'd been reckless and gotten into his share of trouble before the suspension, but once his football dream had been taken away, he'd seemed to lose all sense of self-preservation and self-control. He'd barely gone to class, he'd drunk and smoked and spent more than one night in the town's single jail cell.

Annabelle was sure there were at least three people in town who had also blamed her for all of that—Jackson, his father and his mother. It was possible there were others as well. But no matter what their opinion had been then or was now, it would be very interesting to the town of Bad if Jackson and Annabelle were seen together socially.

"You're asking her out?" Michael asked Jackson. Then he glanced at Annabelle and winced. "Sorry. I don't mean that…it's not that he *shouldn't*…I just didn't know that…"

Clearly Michael was trying not to insult her while still wanting to know what the hell was going on.

Michael was three years older—which probably helped him get along with the guys Annabelle and Jackson's age since he wouldn't have played football against them personally—but even the people of Autre had heard about the big scandal that had rocked Bad football ten years ago. At least one of the Bad boys had lived up to that name that year.

Nice.

"Yes, I'm asking her out," Jackson said. He even raised his voice slightly.

Not that it was necessary. Suddenly it seemed quieter in this section of the coffee shop. Everyone in the near vicinity had heard everything.

That would get the ladies at Bad Hair Day? all riled up. Annabelle was pretty sure the two girls near the window were already putting it on Facebook.

"Um, no." She shook her head. "I mean, no thank you. That's very nice but…"

She couldn't go out with Jackson. The gossip wouldn't be limited to the rehashing of her and Jackson's past together, but would also involve the fact that Jackson was a player—not the football type—and she…wasn't. Everyone knew that Jackson Brady could have any woman he wanted. The stories of his college days had traveled back to Bad and it seemed that he never had a shortage of liquor or women.

Everyone also knew that Annabelle was quiet and kept to herself and loved books more than she loved most people. She was a great teacher. She was animated and engaging and interesting when she was in front of a class talking about a topic she knew and was passionate about. She could also lead and participate in meetings and brainstorming sessions and groups—like her book club. But other than that, she did prefer *not* talking.

They were an unlikely pair even if they didn't have a sordid past together.

The main question on everyone's mind would be "what does Jackson see in her?"

Annabelle glanced at Michael. That was very likely what he was wondering.

But he was looking at her and when their eyes met, he smiled.

Huh, that was more interest than she could remember ever getting from Michael. He was a great guy. Everyone liked him. Annabelle just wasn't his type.

At Brews he always danced with flirtier, funnier women. The ones who could banter with him and make him laugh. Women like her friends Randi, or Sabrina. Confident, sassy women.

"You need to go to dinner with me," Jackson said.

She looked at him. A date with Jackson? The only way it would work would be if it was back in her classroom where she felt comfortable and in control. But now that she'd remembered everything about him and Miss Schneider, that might not be a great idea, either.

"I don't think that's a good idea. But thanks."

He moved in closer. "Can I—" He looked around and then took her arm and pulled her away from the people waiting for their order to be filled and the closest table.

Annabelle went along only because she was not the type to cause a scene. "Mr. Brady, what is going on?"

"You have *got* to stop calling me that." He let go of her, turning to block her between the wall next to the window and his big body. It also effectively blocked her from everyone's view.

Not that they stopped looking.

"You can't call the guy you're dating 'Mr.'"

Her mouth fell open. "I am *not* dating you."

"But I think you should."

He kept his voice low and his body relaxed, but she could see the determination in his eyes.

"That's crazy. I can't think of even one good reason for us to go out."

Except maybe, just maybe, then she could kiss him. Just once. Kissing a guy like Jackson Brady had to be good. By smiling alone he could make her melt a little. Lip to lip…she'd probably lose too many brain cells and find herself unable to remember how to even make a sandwich.

Jackson looked at her for ten heartbeats. Then he stepped close and braced his hand on the wall next to her head. "If you date me, it will be an automatic stamp of approval. It will show everyone that ten years have resulted in growth and maturity and wisdom and I'm no longer that reckless, headstrong kid that tore this town up."

He really did smell good.

She took a long, blatant breath. The way he was standing insinuated an intimacy between them, a willingness to share personal space, that didn't exist. But she didn't feel inclined to push him away.

"You don't need me to date you," she said, also keeping her voice low. "I gave a glowing recommendation to the committee. Once you meet with them, you'll be golden."

"The committee isn't going to meet for at least two weeks. I had a visitor out at Coach's today."

He also had perfect skin. A guy shouldn't get to have skin like that.

"Who?"

"Larry March."

Larry was the president of the school board. She frowned. "What did he say?"

"He told me they weren't going to meet for at least two weeks because they wanted to see how I settled in, watch how things played out, see how the town reacts to me."

"You don't need me," she said again, shaking her head. "You'll be fine with the town. You're helping Coach out and everyone loves him. You and Carter are tight. The whole town likes and respects Carter."

He leaned in and she felt a shiver go through her. A good shiver. A hot shiver.

"Coach has always given me the benefit of the doubt, and Carter and Jase and the other guys are like my band of brothers. Sure, people like them and it will count if they support me, but you, Miss Annabelle... You were not a big fan of mine. In fact, you were my arch nemesis. If you show you've come around, that will be huge."

She pulled in a breath and resisted lifting her hands to her hot cheeks like a blushing schoolgirl. "First of all," she managed, "I was not your arch nemesis. I didn't do what I did because I hated you or wanted to ruin anything for you."

That was the God's honest truth. She hadn't thought her actions through and how they might impact Jackson. In fact, she hadn't really thought they would. He was a kid. A victim in the situation. But he'd ended up suspended from the team. She'd asked herself a thousand times over the years if she would have told Principal Whitacre what she'd seen if she'd known what would happen to Jackson.

She still didn't have an absolute answer to that question.

"And second of all, I can simply tell everyone that I support you being considered for the position."

He leaned back a little. "That's not enough."

"Come on." He was worried, she got that. He really wanted this. "You're the strongest candidate so far."

"So far," he repeated. "Larry said there were two more candidates coming in."

She only knew about one, but that didn't matter. "And if we date, they'll take me off the search committee because of a conflict of interest."

"You don't need to be on the search committee," he said. "You already found me."

That damn grin of his. Wow. He just needed to flash that

around town for a few days. It certainly made her ready to agree to anything he wanted.

"Us dating might keep you from the position. They don't allow staff to date one another."

"We won't be that serious. It will be a little summer fling. Casual. Enough to establish that I'm obviously good enough that the most conservative, well-respected woman in town is willing to spend time with me, but not so much that anyone expects diamond rings and wedding bells."

"I'm the most conservative, well-respected woman in town?" she asked, completely focused on those words. She felt a knot in her stomach. She wasn't sure that was as good a thing as he made it sound.

"Aren't you?" he asked with another grin.

This time her stomach might have flipped, but it might have churned instead. Priscilla Williams, the preacher's grand-daughter and mayor's daughter, *should have* been the most conservative but...Annabelle did probably beat even Cilla. Even before Cilla hooked up with Jase Hawkins. One of Bad's best bad boys. And a good friend of Jackson's, as a matter of fact.

Annabelle felt a little sick. Being the most conservative woman in town might be the reason she hadn't had any hot dates...or any dates at all...in...ever.

Conservative and well-respected? And who else was conservative and well-respected? Nuns. And spinsters.

She put her hands on his chest and pushed him back. "You know what they call conservative and well-respected women?" she asked.

"What?"

"Single."

She stomped out of the coffee shop and headed for her yoga class. The lemon poppy seed muffin was for later but the coffee she needed *now*. And fortunately it had been cooling off long enough that she could chug it.

CHAPTER
THREE

YOGA PANTS. Yep, that was something else he liked women in. Jeans, short skirts, yoga pants or nothing at all.

And that long, flowy skirt from the other day had been covering up some nice stuff.

Jackson watched Annabelle flounce to the door and then down the sidewalk past the huge coffee shop window.

Damn.

Even as she was prissy-flouncing, those yoga pants definitely added a mark in the pro column for dating her.

He smiled at everyone in the tiny coffee shop, knowing that they had all taken in the interaction between him and Annabelle. They hadn't overheard the conversation, but they'd seen them together. That was all he needed right now.

He stepped out onto the sunny sidewalk and pulled on his sunglasses. He'd done morning chores at Coach's and he now had a break before he needed to get out there for afternoon work. Perfect time to stop by the real estate office and see if there was any land for sale.

"What the hell are you doing?" Carter fell into step beside Jackson.

Jackson looked at his friend. Carter looked impressive in his cop uniform, but it made Jackson chuckle. Carter had hardly been an angel growing up.

"Uh, see you guys later," Michael gave them both a quick wave and started in the opposite direction.

"Where're you goin'?" Jackson called after him.

"Away from your best friend kickin' your ass for messin' with a nice girl like AJ," Michael said, stopping by his truck.

Jackson looked at Carter. "Is that what you're doin'?"

"Maybe. Michael filled me in. You asked her out?"

Jackson glanced back at Michael, but the other man had already started his truck. "Why's he think he needs to tell you about that?"

"Maybe he was just tellin' me the morning gossip from the coffee shop as we ran into each other on the sidewalk," Carter said. "Should he be *worried* about it?"

"He seemed...surprised." And a little interested. Not in the conversation between Jackson and Annabelle, but in *Annabelle*. Which had made a weird possessiveness streak through Jackson that he didn't really want to admit to. Not to himself. And certainly not to Carter.

"You asked *AJ Hartington* out."

He really hated the AJ thing. It didn't fit. Jackson stopped walking and faced his friend. "Yeah, I was there. *So?*"

"She's not exactly...your type."

"She's beautiful and smart. You're sayin' I go for ugly, dumb girls?"

"But she doesn't like you."

"I don't think that's entirely true." He really didn't. He thought it was possible that Annabelle might even be surprised by how much she liked him.

She'd been impressed by his farm at least. It was a start, which meant it was an opportunity. He was great at capitalizing on opportunities.

"But she's..." Carter seemed to be casting around for the proper adjective. "Stiff."

Jackson cocked an eyebrow. "Stiff?"

"Uptight, cool." Carter shrugged. "She doesn't date."

"She has a tattoo." Why had he said that? It didn't have anything to do with what Carter was talking about. Or did it?

Carter's eyes widened. "What?"

Jackson nodded. It wasn't like a tattoo said anything specific about a person. Tattoos could mean a lot of different things. Maybe Annabelle's had been a drunken mistake or something. But it still represented the fact that there were things about her that would surprise people.

Clearly.

Carter seemed to be thinking about that. "What is it? And where?"

"A music thingy. A symbol. On her foot."

"Huh."

"So there might be some things you don't know about her."

Carter frowned. "Huh."

"Anyway, why do you care? I asked her out. Nothing to do with you. Or LeClaire." All these other men needed to not be thinking about Annabelle so much in his opinion.

"Annabelle's a really nice person. Friends with a lot of the other women in our friend group. I'm just sayin' you better watch yourself."

Jackson frowned. "Or what? You're gonna do something?" What the fuck? Was Carter warning him off of Annabelle?

Carter chuckled. "I won't need to. Randi and Sabrina and Daisy and Regan will make you disappear, and I'll never find a trace of evidence."

Okay, so the Bad girls could be...a handful too. Those four in particular could probably make him pretty sorry if they wanted to. "How hard would you investigate any foul play?" Jackson asked his cop friend.

"About as hard as you'd deserve," Carter said. Then he chuckled and slapped Jackson on the shoulder. "Relax. You don't need to kiss up to Annabelle to get in good with the search committee. You've got this."

"Am I that obvious?"

"Uh, yeah."

Jackson sighed.

"Relax, man. Be yourself. They'd be stupid not to choose you."

"Thanks." Jackson did appreciate the vote of confidence and hopefully Carter was right. Jackson's resume should speak for itself. He was proud of who he'd become and the things he'd done since leaving Bad. Minus those first couple of years, of course.

Carter headed toward his patrol car and Jackson walked the three blocks to the real estate office.

"Jackson."

"Hey, Tom."

It was a small office, like everything in Bad, and Tom Thorpe, the large-land agent in the area, greeted Jackson personally.

"What brings you in here?" Tom rose and extended his hand to Jackson.

The two men shook and Tom gestured to the chair in front of his desk. Jackson sat on the edge, his elbows on his thighs.

"I'm looking into buying some land in the area. Just curious about any listings you have at the moment."

Tom covered well, but Jackson could tell he was surprised. "Buying land, huh? That's a big step."

"I own about two hundred acres in Nebraska. We do vegetables, have fruit trees, some livestock, eggs and just got into honeybees last summer."

Tom looked intrigued. "So why are you looking here?"

Jackson tried to keep his easygoing smile and posture in place but he couldn't help feeling instantly defensive. He knew it was an overreaction. Tom was just asking what any realtor would ask. "I'm staying in Bad. I'm helping Coach out and hope to help out at the high school in the fall with some counseling."

Tom nodded. "I heard that you were interested in that position. But owning land is a bit bigger commitment, don't you think?"

And *that* was why he'd felt defensive. Jackson had known Tom would question his level of commitment. He hadn't expected it to be out loud, necessarily, but his reputation wasn't exactly solid when it came to fulfilling his obligations.

Sure it was unprofessional, rude even, of Tom to insinuate that Jackson didn't know what he was doing. But Tom was one of the older generation, life-long Bad residents who was unquestionably loyal to and protective of the town.

Jackson didn't quite catch his frown in time, but he smoothed it almost immediately. "Yes it is. But this is home. I need to stick around and I have a passion for self-sufficient farming."

"Is that right? How much acreage are you looking at?"

"I'm thinking a hundred or so. With room to expand."

Tom's eyes widened. "That's...a lot."

Jackson consciously unclenched his fist. "It is. But I want to put in fruit trees and have some pastureland."

"How do you think you're going to be able to run that size of an operation and work at the school?" Tom asked.

It wouldn't matter if he was working at the school or not. A one hundred-acre self-sufficient homestead would take a lot more hands than his.

Not that any of this was Tom's business. He was a real estate agent. Jackson wanted some real estate. Tom should have been thrilled at the thought of his commission from this sale.

"In Nebraska, I run the farm with a bunch of kids."

"Kids?"

"Teens, young adults. Kids who were in trouble and needed to learn about hard work and purpose." Jackson was unable to keep the pride out of his voice. "It's a helluva operation."

"And that's what you're thinking about here?"

"I'd love to do that here. I love the life on a self-sustaining farm for myself too, but the effect it all has on the kids is amazing. I've written a few papers on it, presented about it at conferences."

Who would have ever thought Jackson Brady, hell-raiser, would present to the American Psychological Association?

"Is that right?"

Clearly not Tom Thorpe.

"It is," Jackson repeated calmly. He knew he shouldn't care what his tiny hometown thought of him. Hell, he'd brought all of it on himself and he'd known it, even at the time.

He knew who he was now and was proud of his accomplishments.

But he did care. Not just because of the job, either. He wanted to show them all that he had changed.

Because then maybe he could fully, finally, believe that himself.

He felt different. He knew on the outside he seemed different. He'd changed his life, his habits, his attitudes.

But there was undeniably a part of him that wasn't completely convinced he wasn't just covering it all up. Maybe all of that rebellion and fuck-it-who-cares was just under the surface and one day it would rise up and take over again.

"You're thinking about bringing some troubled kids to town, then?" Tom asked, not even bothering to hide what he clearly felt about that.

Jackson didn't hide his frown this time, either. "This is a fantastic little town," he said. "The kids I've worked with have been from all walks of life and backgrounds, but a place like this, where people are friendly and honest and hardworking, would have a tremendous impact on them." He meant that. The farm in Nebraska had done wonders for the kids. Giving them a safe place with boundaries, full acceptance and a chance to truly be a part of something. It had been life changing for many of them. But Jackson was intrigued by the idea of bringing some kids from the city, probably New Orleans, to a town like Bad. The sense of community was bigger. The idea that even more people could accept and support them, believe in them—that had all kinds of potential.

Though judging by Tom's reaction, it might not be as easy as it sounded.

Jackson just wasn't sure if it was the "troubled kids" that bothered Tom or if it was the idea that Jackson was driving this particular bus.

"Don't you think it might be a good idea to settle in a bit first? See if things are going to work out? Before you make a big investment," Tom finally said.

Jackson swallowed back his first reaction. So this was how it was going to be. Great. Good to know. "You know, Tom, maybe I'll just take a drive around, talk to some folks." He rose from the chair. "This is Bad. If someone's selling something, I'll probably have good luck down at the diner."

Tom's jaw clenched. Probably thinking about the six percent he might be giving up. "I just don't think you want to rush into anything."

"I understand. I appreciate your concern for me." Jackson was sure that his sarcasm was apparent.

He left Tom's office, emotions churning through his gut—anger, disbelief, frustration and maybe just a touch of despair. Was he going to be able to do this? He wanted to stay. It was time for him to give back.

But his friendly, hardworking, honest hometown was going to have to give him a fucking break.

———

The people of Bad loved a reason to get dressed up and go out and when there wasn't a good reason, they made one up. "Goin' Out" was like a weekly national holiday—everyone had it on their calendars and observed it with great celebration. It could occur anywhere from the town park to the football field to Bad Brews but it occurred. All the time.

If you asked anyone in Bad what they were doing on Friday night, the answer was always "goin' out".

It was not the most comfortable place to live for a girl who preferred books to people and music she made herself. Yet, it was home and she couldn't imagine living and teaching anywhere else. So Annabelle put up with it and she made herself socialize once in a while to keep everyone happy.

Okay, to keep her mother happy. Which kept her father happy, which kept Annabelle happy.

It was a delicate balance that she'd finally found and she now maintained it carefully. If she went out once a month, she only had to hear about how she was going to die alone and only ever give her mom and dad grandcats every other month or so.

Strangely enough, Annabelle didn't have any cats. Still, that was her mother's favorite line. Avoiding that line this week was Annabelle's reason for being at Brews on Monday night.

"Whew, I love dancing with that man." Miranda Doyle slid onto the stool opposite Annabelle at the tall round table they'd claimed at the edge of the dance floor. She lifted her mane of long dark hair, letting the back of her neck cool. She'd been dancing with Michael. Annabelle had been watching.

It felt as if Annabelle was always watching. She was also nursing a strawberry daiquiri, heavy on the strawberry and light on everything else.

It wasn't that she didn't like the taste of liquor, rum in particular, but she didn't like feeling fuzzy-headed. She knew some people drank specifically for that effect. She, on the other hand, loved having her faculties completely clear. Plus, liquor made her tired and she was at a good point in the book she was reading and she wanted to stay up long enough when she got home to finish the chapter.

Annabelle didn't have to look around to see that Michael already had someone new on the dance floor dancing to Brett Eldredge's *Beat of the Music*. Or rather, someone new had *him* on the dance floor. Annabelle was certainly not the only woman in town who noticed Chief LeClaire. Part of his appeal, of course, was that he wasn't from here. There was something fun about flirting with someone you hadn't known since Kindergarten. But there was no denying that it was also *him*. He was handsome, and charming, and never said no to any woman who asked him to dance, and when he had a woman on the dance floor, he was fully focused on her alone.

Annabelle sighed. Obviously, if she asked him to dance, he'd say yes. Obviously, he'd pay attention and make conversation. She could get to know him better. She could see if there was *any* spark. So why wasn't she asking?

"I love your hair like that," Randi commented, studying Annabelle across the table.

"Really?" Annabelle fingered the twist she'd tried tonight.

She'd never been one to fuss with her hair. She had thick, naturally curly hair which, in Louisiana, meant she had big, frizzy hair a lot of the time. She preferred to wear it up or pulled back so she didn't have to mess with it. Ponytails and French braids were perfect.

When she went out, though, she tried to put a little effort in. She got on Pinterest and searched for hairstyles every month and it did give her a little boost of confidence when one worked. Which was about fifty percent of the time.

"That's a good one," Randi said with a nod.

"And I'm wearing my boots." Annabelle stuck a foot out from under the table.

Randi grinned. "I noticed. I like them."

Annabelle smiled. She didn't care for boots as a general rule. But she loved the color of these. The deep red made her feel daring.

It was crazy. Annabelle hadn't been daring for a second in her whole life. Miranda, on the other hand, personified daring. Miranda was nothing like Annabelle.

More specifically Annabelle was nothing like Randi.

Since coming home to Bad, Annabelle had reconnected with

some of the girls from high school and had, surprisingly, become friends with them. That had led to Annabelle knowing more about makeup, hair, and footwear than she'd ever imagined. Or wanted. "Hey, you got new lipstick," she commented.

Randi smiled. "Isn't it great?"

"Love it."

"You should try it." Randi held it out.

She shook her head. "I'm fine."

"Honey, lipstick can do *almost* as much as underwear for your self-confidence."

Annabelle laughed and shook her head. Randi maintained that a woman's words and actions were dictated by how she perceived herself, and her self-perception came from her underwear.

All of her friends were gorgeous, confident, comfortable in their own skins.

Annabelle wanted some of that.

She studied her friend as Randi applied the lipstick and wondered for the thousandth time why they were friends. Randi was gorgeous and sexy and had tons of male attention constantly, but she was also a bit of a tomboy and a complete football freak. She knew and followed everything about the game, from the pros to college to high school. She had a particular obsession for high school football right here in Bad though. She'd been the head cheerleader in high school and she'd lived for cheering on the sidelines.

Annabelle had never been to a football game, Bad or otherwise.

She'd been aware of the championship season and the Big Win their senior year simply because she hadn't been living under a rock. There had been no missing the brightly painted windows on every business in town, the pep rallies, the decorated hallways at school, the pep rallies, the local news coverage on TV, radio, and in the paper, oh, and she couldn't forget the pep rallies.

It had seemed as though there was another one every other day and Randi had been at the forefront, reveling in the attention and the hype.

The two women had had nothing in common growing up and even now they were very different. But Randi was one of the two local mechanics at Bad Brakes and she was the only thing standing between Annabelle's yellow VW bug, Darcy—yes, named for the hero in Jane Austen's *Pride and Prejudice*—and death. Annabelle and Darcy made near-monthly trips to Randi's shop. If she didn't know better, Annabelle would think Darcy had a crush on Randi.

Randi turned and looked over her shoulder toward the bar, then back to Annabelle. "I heard you got asked to dinner."

Annabelle frowned and glanced in the same direction.

Jackson Brady was standing at the bar. Looking gorgeous. And big.

It had been three days since she'd seen him at Bad Habit and he'd asked her out.

She hadn't stopped thinking about it since.

A jolt of awareness shot through her as her gaze swept over him from head to toe and back again. Twice. He really was *big*. He had been a football star, which required some size, but he'd been their running back. Running backs had to be tough and solid, but also agile. And fast. With his wide shoulder, narrow hips and tight glutes, he had been nearly unstoppable.

She hadn't needed to go to games to hear all about *that*.

"Annabelle?"

His abs were clearly rock solid even with a cotton shirt covering them. The button-down shirt was plain white and he'd paired it with jeans. The collar was open and he had the sleeves pushed up on his forearms. He looked casual, but completely hot. The chest and stomach behind the shirt had to be—

"AJ!" Randi snapped her fingers in front of Annabelle's nose.

She jerked back, her attention fully on the woman in front of her again. "What?"

"You were nearly drooling."

Annabelle cleared her throat. "What were we talking about?"

"That Jackson Brady asked you to dinner."

"Oh. Well, that doesn't matter."

Randi gave her a sly smile. "Oh, I think it matters a lot. Even more so now that I see the way you're blushing."

Annabelle put a hand to her cheek. "I'm not blushing." But she definitely was.

"Why did you say no?" Randi asked. She was blatantly checking Jackson out. "I'd be all over that."

"He only asked me to dinner to butter me up and make sure I said nice things about him to the search committee."

"Who cares *why* he did it? He asked. All you have to do is say yes." Randi lifted her beer and drank, letting that sink in.

He had asked. Annabelle hadn't been asked out since she'd moved back to Bad. She'd always planned to come back to Bad, but she did miss the city. She'd found people like her there, for the first time, and she'd been able to fully be herself. There were other people who were satisfied to simply sit in a coffee shop and talk books. There were other people who chose a small independent theater production over going to a club. There were other people who preferred to spend hours in their own company and absolute quiet.

She'd even dated. A cellist, a photographer, an organic farmer who made his own soap, and a tattoo artist.

Artists, intellectuals, free spirits.

She'd been completely comfortable there. She knew what made those people tick and she could relate to them. It was a lot like how she felt in her classroom. That was her turf, it was familiar, nothing would come up that she didn't know or couldn't handle.

Then she'd come back to Bad to teach English and American Literature.

She questioned that decision on a near-weekly basis. But her life here was simple and quiet and rewarding in its own way.

There just weren't many tattoo artists and cellists here.

No, Bad was full of hard-working blue-collar guys—ranchers and fishermen and mechanics and cops and firemen. It wasn't as if the city didn't have some of those guys too, but they weren't everywhere she turned. She'd been able to cocoon herself in a world she understood, a world where *she* was popular.

Bad was overrun with testosterone.

She didn't do as well with testosterone. She couldn't talk about ranching, or football, or hunting, or four-wheeling.

She was completely intimidated and overwhelmed by guys from Bad.

Guys like Jackson Brady. And Michael LeClaire.

"Let's say for two seconds that I thought going out with Jackson might be fun," she said. There had been an inexplicable, completely unexpected chemistry between them in her classroom the first day and again that morning in the coffee shop. So there was potential there. But... "What would we talk about? We have nothing in common."

Randi waved that away, clearly unconcerned. "You talk about school. You talk about people you know from high school. You ask him about his arrest record." She gave Annabelle a big grin. "I'm guessing Jackson Brady has some very interesting stories. And you know as well as I do that men love to talk about themselves. Just keep asking him questions all night."

Annabelle's eyes again went to Michael. The blonde was totally into him—or acting like it anyway—and it was working. He was running his hand up and down her back, he was whispering in her ear and moving his hips against hers. Sure, they were dancing, and he could say those hip swivels were in time to the music, but it was obvious the music didn't matter.

Michael was an EMT and Annabelle had once entertained the idea of pretending to get faint one night in Brews so he'd come to her rescue and check her out, but she'd chickened out doing even that. How did she expect to get his attention when she was constantly telling herself he was out of her league and that she couldn't keep up with him?

Her gaze bounced back to Jackson. He was talking and laughing, looking comfortable, sexy, but…strangely approachable.

She could actually imagine walking up to him and asking *him* to dance.

This was the guy who had hated her for years. The guy who she'd ruined. She knew he'd walked on as a freshman at his college's football program, but hadn't played much. She knew he'd gotten kicked off the team for partying and reckless behavior. She knew that, because of those run-ins, he would have a hard time being trusted around the kids here.

But he'd walked into her classroom and faced her, had been humble enough to acknowledge that her opinion and recommendation were important. He'd come back, in spite of the fact Coach Karr had kicked him off the team, to help Coach when he needed him. He had not just finished school and gotten a good job, he'd made something of himself and turned things around to help kids who were in trouble. He was facing the town he'd let down.

And he was standing at the bar, looking relaxed and sure of himself, laughing and chatting as if he belonged and wanted to be a part of the community again.

She could imagine crossing the bar and asking him to dance.

She wouldn't even need sexy underwear on to do it.

And now, looking at Jackson, a part of her suddenly wanted to go shopping at Victoria's Secret.

She needed to feel sexy, to come off as sexy. She needed to come off as sexy to get Michael's attention. She needed to get Michael's attention if she wanted to start dating him, and she needed to start dating him if she wanted to have a relationship with him.

No, he wasn't a professor or a cellist, but he was the only guy in the parish she was attracted to.

Annabelle glanced at Jackson again.

Okay, Michael was one of *two* men in the parish she was attracted to.

Randi must have read the intent in Annabelle's eyes, because she handed over the lipstick with a grin.

CHAPTER
FOUR

"HI, JACKSON."

Annabelle's soft voice behind him felt as if she'd stroked her hand down his arm. Every muscle in his arm and his stomach tightened. And maybe a couple a little lower.

From a simple *hi*?

That reaction definitely drew Jackson's attention from the conversation at the bar. It had been mostly small talk, a few questions about Coach, and him trying to nonchalantly feel people out about any land for sale. Not to mention trying, unsuccessfully, to work his desire to bring some of the city teens to Bad into the conversation. He needed to know if Tom was the only one who was against the idea or if that was going to rile up everyone.

But the moment Annabelle said, "Hi, Jackson", he forgot about everything but wanting to know how her hair smelled. Again.

He turned to face her fully.

Damn, she looked good.

That was the thought that first hit him. And it was strange. She was wearing one of those full skirts again that didn't show a thing. But the image of her in yoga pants was branded on his brain and he could easily conjure it.

The memory made him grin. "Hey, Annabelle."

She took a deep breath and looked, if he wasn't mistaken, a little shy. "I was wondering if you'd dance with me."

Dance with her? Oh, really?

"I've never ever turned down the chance to have a beautiful woman in my arms," he said.

She flushed and Jackson almost grinned in satisfaction. He did so love making women blush and with Annabelle it seemed so easy. But he couldn't quite grin. He was working too hard on not giving away how much he wanted to have her up against him.

What the hell was going on?

She smiled and the feeling got stronger.

"Great." She started for the dance floor without waiting for him.

Jackson took a second to watch her go and changed his mind about not liking the flowing skirts. They weren't as good as yoga pants or nothing at all, of course, but there was something about the way the silky material draped over her hips and swung against then away from the curve of her ass that made a man's heart rate pick up.

It was kind of like the difference between flirting and outright telling a guy *I want you.*

The blatant was very, very nice. But a good flirtation was equally compelling once in a while.

Jackson glanced at the other men at the bar. None were watching Annabelle walk away.

That was good.

He thought he might want to keep the secret of Annabelle's cute butt to himself.

Jesus. Cute butt?

Jackson started after her. When she got to the edge of the

dance floor, she swung to face him and the skirt swirled around her.

Jackson noticed her boots immediately. Annabelle had spent her teen years in tennis shoes but tonight she was wearing red cowboy boots. She really was full of surprises.

"Damn. Was hoping to catch a glimpse of that music thing again." He stepped close and held out his arms, palms up, ready to two-step her around to some old George Strait.

"Music thing?"

"Your tattoo."

"The one on my foot?"

He lifted an eyebrow. "Is there another one?" *Oh, damn, please let there be another one.*

"There is. In fact, there are several more."

Yes. Now to convince her to show him where. "Several?"

She grinned. "Yes."

She still wasn't getting closer. He wiggled his fingers. "I'm not used to women taking so much time to get up against me," he told her. "I feel like a dumbass here, Annabelle. Come on."

She blinked, then seemed to register what he was talking about. She laughed, said, "Sorry," and stepped into his arms.

His hand settled on her lower back, hers on his shoulder as he took her other hand in his. They began moving in the steps that every kid in Bad knew from the time they could walk. A two-step was right up there with learning that hot sauce goes on everything and when your grandmother told you something, the correct response was always, "Yes, ma'am."

As they stepped around the dancefloor, he just looked at her. Annabelle Hartington smelled like strawberries.

Finally she asked, "What?"

"Shh," he told her. "I'm imagining your other tattoos."

She looked startled for a moment, then her face relaxed into a knowing smile that women have been giving men since the Garden of Eden. It was a mix of fake innocence and I've-got-you-right-where-I-want-you.

Which made something hot throb deep inside Jackson. He was right where she wanted him? She wanted him *anywhere*?

"What about them?" she asked sweetly.

But he was starting to suspect there was a spicy side to Annabelle.

He tightened the arm around her, pulling her closer. "What they are. Where they are."

She licked her bottom lip. "Why don't you just ask me?"

"My imagination is a lot of fun."

He was flirting with her. That wasn't exactly a shock. Jackson usually had to try *not* to flirt when he was dancing with women in bars.

No, the surprising thing was that Annabelle seemed to realize it.

She certainly didn't strike him as the flirtatious party-girl type. Yet there was a recognition in her eyes that said she knew exactly what was going on.

And didn't mind a bit.

Annabelle tipped her head to one side, her lips curled in a soft smile and her body moved closer to his as the song switched to Ashley McBryde's *One Night Standards*.

"I can almost guarantee," she said softly, "that you will never guess what the others are. And you will probably only guess *where* about half of them are."

Flirting had just ratcheted up to seduction. He was pretty sure. That's how this felt, anyway. The only thing making him wonder was the fact that this was Annabelle.

"How many are we talking?"

"Eight."

He knew his eyes went wide. "You have eight tattoos?"

She nodded. "Seven besides the one you've seen."

Of course they could be tiny. Little daisies didn't need to take up a lot of skin. But eight?

He'd dated women with tattoos before. Lots of them, in some cases. They were gorgeous and sexy and he loved them.

But there was something very sweetly sexy about Annabelle having seven other hidden tattoos that he really, really liked. Maybe it was because it was unexpected. But he thought maybe it was more that these tattoos were obviously only for her. She hadn't done it to be sexy—especially if the majority were hidden. She'd done it because she wanted to. They would say something about her.

He liked that most of all. And he *really* wanted to know what they were now.

His grip on her hand tightened and he dropped his voice to a husky growl. "I think instead of guessing, I'd rather go on a treasure hunt."

Her lips parted and she sucked in a little breath. He couldn't hear it over the noise in the bar, of course, but he could see it.

"That brings up something I'd like to talk to you about."

"Yes."

She raised an eyebrow. "You don't know what it is."

"It has to do with your tattoos, I'm in."

That seemed to please her, but it was the God's honest truth. He wanted, *needed*, to know more about those tattoos.

"I changed my mind about what you asked me at the coffee shop."

Jackson stopped dancing and looked down at her. "About dinner?"

"About the whole thing. The dating thing."

Now *this* was very interesting. He'd been planning to bring it up again. After they'd danced a little longer and he had her blushing and laughing a little more and maybe breathing a little harder. He'd had it all planned out. So this was a surprise.

He nodded. "That's great. But you should know that I don't want it to be fake. I want to date you for real. I'm done lying to my friends."

Now why had he said that? He had turned over a new leaf and was upfront and honest with the people in his life, but taking her to dinner a few times, maybe sending her flowers once or twice, and kissing her in the town square would have sufficed. He'd told her earlier that it would be a fling—just enough to show the town that she thought he was a good guy.

But looking down at her now, he wanted more than dinner.

That was stupid, no doubt. But again, this was an opportunity not to be wasted.

She licked her bottom lip.

Oh, yeah, he wasn't going to waste this.

"You want to actually date for the summer?" she asked.

"Yes."

"What does that entail exactly?"

He would very happily give her a list. And the list involved a lot of naked time suddenly.

It was crazy. Women had been the last thing on his mind when he came back to Bad. He dated. Absolutely. But he hadn't left a serious girlfriend behind, nor had he brought one with him. There would be no one coming to Bad trying to find him or crying into her pillow in Omaha missing him. He'd never had trouble getting female attention. But he had a tendency to hang out with women who were like him—intense, driven, with hot tempers and who had a hard time seeing the long-term consequences of their actions. He grinned thinking about it. He'd had some seriously crazy relationships. They were fun, hot, consuming...and over quickly.

It was like a bar fight—the adrenaline pumped, he got to feel like a big shot, he got a little sore, and then it was over and he moved on.

"Are you okay?"

The soft voice pulled him from his thoughts and he realized he'd been grinning like an idiot over seemingly nothing. He took her hand and pulled her across the dance floor to the less crowded area near the back exit.

"I'm fine."

Annabelle was about as different from the women he usually dated as he could have found. It was perfect. He could use a change of pace, something new. He was always encouraging the kids to look beyond what they thought they wanted and had always had. Repeating the same patterns over and over—even the ones that always produced bad results—was the easy way to go and the reason most people never got out of their ruts, including the self-destructive ones. He truly believed that often the best things were right outside of a person's comfort zone.

If he wanted the town to look at him differently, he needed to give them something new and different to look at. The women he was usually attracted to would not feel new to Bad.

Annabelle was new though. And the attraction thing was not going to be a problem.

"Did you change your mind?"

"About dating you?" He chuckled. "Not at all."

They had to stand close together to be heard over the music and conversation around them, but it was quieter over here, and people would be able to see them together but not eavesdrop on their conversation.

"Good. Because there's something I want to get out of it too."

That, too, was very interesting. "Really? Like what?"

She took a deep breath and focused on his chin rather than his eyes. "It was what you said earlier about me being the most conservative woman in town."

Right. The thing that had pissed her off in the coffee shop. "I'm sorry if that hurt your feelings."

In his mind it was a *good* thing, but she had clearly been upset.

"It isn't your fault," she said. "It's true."

Her voice was softer now and he moved closer to be sure he heard. "And that's a bad thing?"

It was a fantastic thing, from where he was standing. Annabelle was not only a good girl, a nice girl, a smart girl— he'd dated very few of any of those girls and he'd never dated one that was a combination of all three—she was also bright and independent. The town would have to believe he'd won her over to get her to go out with him. A woman like Annabelle didn't get swept up in things like him being a hell of a good time or up for anything in the bedroom. A woman like Annabelle didn't get swept up at all. She made good, rational decisions based on information and proof—not adrenaline and lust.

Frankly, adrenaline and lust were two of his favorite things.

Exactly why he needed *less* of both in his life.

"I think I need to be less…like that." She focused on something over his shoulder and Jackson turned to find what it was.

Or who it was.

He couldn't tell. The room was full, the dance floor covered.

He looked at her again. "What's going through that pretty head?"

She met his eyes. "You're not the only guy here who thinks that. I want to show the men around here that I'm not uptight and unapproachable."

Ah, this was making a little more sense now.

"Done." He wanted to date her. For his reputation. And a bunch of other things that were as surprising as they were sudden. But if there was a reason she wanted to date him too— and it involved her *not* being uptight— damn right he was all in.

Her eyes widened and her cheeks flushed.

God, he wanted to kiss her. Badly. That wasn't an uncommon urge when standing close to a beautiful woman, of course. He had a very healthy libido—maybe too healthy sometimes. He found all kinds of women attractive and often felt desire and lust. But with Annabelle it felt different. He couldn't just push her up against the wall and go for it. He needed a little finesse, would have to work up to it, would have to—

She gripped the front of his shirt and pulled him in, going up on tiptoe and pressing her mouth to his.

Or he could just push her up against the wall and go for it.

Opportunity.

That was what this was.

He tunneled both hands into her hair, pulling it from the fancy twist. Then he tipped her head and took control.

Her lips were tight, hardly letting him feel or taste her. Her body was tight against his too, but not in the good way.

That wasn't a problem.

Jackson put a hand on her hip, squeezing and caressing her skin through the soft material of her skirt. He felt some of the tension ease and he gentled the pressure of the kiss and opened his lips slightly, urging her to do the same. Her hand tightened on his shirt, but her lips parted.

He licked along her bottom lip slowly, tasting her, letting her get used to the feel. She sighed and her lips opened farther.

He pulled his fingers through her hair. The strands slid over the back of his hand and fingers like silk, and as if he'd scratched a scratch-and-sniff sticker, the scent of strawberries grew stronger around him.

And it made him hungry.

She sighed and her mouth opened even more, her body relaxing against him. Jackson walked her the four short steps to the wall and pressed her against it, running his hand from her hip, around her waist and up her back.

She was slender and soft and warm and his hands itched to feel more of her.

But it wasn't until she unclenched her fist and let go of his shirt to move her hand up his chest to the back of his neck, and then into his hair, that he opened his mouth and swept his tongue in over hers.

The resulting moan from her shot a dose of need into his bloodstream. Suddenly it became all about getting her to make that sound again. Over and over.

The kiss turned hot.

Her tongue moved against his, not timidly as he would have expected, but bold and hot. Her hands both clasped the back of his head and she arched against him. She was too short to line up their good parts perfectly, but he got the gist.

And wanted more.

He lifted his head, breathing hard and staring into her eyes.

"We need to get out of here."

She pressed her lips together and nodded.

Decision made. He let her go, took her hand and headed for the door, pulling her along behind him.

They got looks, that was for sure, but unlike his usual reckless, there's-time-for-consequences-later, he knew exactly what he was doing. He was taking Annabelle Hartington parking. And he wanted everyone to know it.

CHAPTER
FIVE

ANNABELLE HAD NEVER KISSED a guy in public.

She wasn't sure she'd ever kissed a guy like she'd kissed Jackson.

Okay, Jackson had kissed her. She might have initiated it, but he had definitely taken over. And *no one* had ever kissed her like that.

A flash of pleasure went through her. She knew everyone was staring at them as Jackson pulled her through the room toward the door. She knew what they were all thinking. And she loved it.

At the moment, they were all questioning what she was thinking. This was Jackson Brady. Even without their history, the town knew Jackson as a wild child and Annabelle as the ultimate good girl.

But she was fully depending on her good girl persona to meet and maybe exceed Jackson's bad boy reputation. His was engrained in their memories, but the fact that he'd come home to help Coach had already put a crack in their strongly held opinions of him.

Nothing had cracked her uptight, conservative reputation.

Yet.

She tripped along behind him over the gravel of the parking lot. When they stopped next to a deep-purple '69 Pontiac GTO and he dug his keys out of his pocket, she caught her breath. This was his?

Jackson heard her little gasp.

He hadn't looked at her since he'd said they needed to leave. Now he glanced from her to the car and back.

"What?"

She ran her hand over the hood of the car. "She's gorgeous."

Jackson was clearly surprised. "You like?"

She looked up at him. The car was beautiful. He'd obviously paid a lot to have it restored and took excellent care of it, but she loved that he also drove it. A car like this needed to be on the road.

"I love her." Her eyes widened. "Ooh, could I drive?"

Jackson looked like she'd asked him if he knew how to get to Mars. "Um, no."

"Oh, come on, I'm a great driver." Of course, in a car like this she might be tempted to press on the gas a little harder than usual. But a deep-purple '69 GTO was not made for going fifty-five.

He turned to face her fully, arms crossed. "You seriously want to drive my car?"

"I do."

His gaze dropped to her lips. "If I let you drive, what do I get?"

"Whatever you want." She meant it. She wanted to drive this car.

And she wanted to give Jackson whatever he wanted.

The whole dating thing was a means to an end—for both of them—but it wasn't as if she didn't think she was going to enjoy every second of it.

"You should be careful saying things like that to a guy you don't know very well." Jackson's voice was deeper, rougher.

"Why?" she asked. "I want to shed this conservative, Sunday-school-teacher thing. If *you* look at me differently, other people will look at me differently too."

"You want other people to look at you differently?" he asked, clearly not buying it.

"I want the guys around here to look at me differently."

"Which guys?"

"The ones like you. The ones who think I'm a goody two-shoes and wouldn't touch a conservative, uptight bookworm. The ones who don't think I know how to have fun."

Jackson was scowling now. "Wouldn't you rather date guys who *do* like conserva—" He broke off when he saw her frown. "Men who *appreciate* women like you?" he amended.

"But that's the thing— none of you really know me, do you?"

She wasn't sure exactly where the bravado was coming from but she thought maybe the car next to her had something to do with it. She still had her hand resting on the hood and it did make her heart beat a little faster. It was exactly the kind of car she wanted to own, but didn't have the guts for. It was the kind of car that made everyone take notice. It was the kind of car that made you want to say, "fuck it, let's go".

And Annabelle could count on one hand the number of times she'd even said the word "fuck" in her life.

She wanted a car like this in her garage.

And the fact that Jackson Brady had shown up in Bad in this car felt like it meant something.

Something good.

She'd take a royal purple '69 GTO over a white horse any damn day.

He looked at her for another long moment. "You might be right about that," he finally said. "I would have never guessed you have a thing for cars."

She nodded, her attention on the car again. "I know nothing about them except how they look and feel and smell."

"Feel and smell?"

"I love the feel of a rumbling engine, the feel of a sudden acceleration, the feel of the leather seats, the *smell* of the leather seats and the oil and the exhaust."

"Damn, girl," he said, his voice low and growly like before. "That's more of a turn on than those yoga pants."

She raised her eyes to his. "My yoga pants?"

"You looked good leaving me."

She had? No kidding. She grinned up at him. "I might look even better coming."

He didn't say anything, but he growled again and moved into her personal space quickly.

That was *definitely* the car. She lifted her hand as if the hood was suddenly hot and gave a shaky laugh. "Hot cars make me feel brave."

"I like it. I really fucking like it."

She stepped away from the car and from him. "On second thought…"

On second thought, she was in way over her head. What was she thinking? She couldn't *date* Jackson Brady. This car was the embodiment of all the reasons why—it was great to look at, made her want to go fast and hard, and was infinitely dangerous. She wanted *a little* of that in her life. Not full time and not at the dosages Jackson represented.

"Hang on." He snagged her wrist and tugged her close again.

She cast a longing look at the car.

"We need to talk," he said, moving to open the car door. "Get in."

"I…shouldn't."

Of course he noticed her hesitation.

He shifted so she was in front of him and nudged her forward toward the car. "You know you want to," he said softly.

His low voice in her ear seemed to rumble through her body, waking up nerve endings all over and making them sigh.

She did want to. And it only had a little to do with the car.

She stepped forward, feeling as though she was being

tempted by the devil himself. Stay or go? Stay and regret it or go and...regret it? He'd said they needed to talk. She knew that wasn't all that was going to happen if she got into that car.

The scent of leather wafted out.

Damn. She was going in.

She sat down and started to reach for the steering wheel but Jackson climbed in after her, scooting her over to the edge of the bucket seat.

"I thought you said I could drive."

"I wanted to be sure you would let me come along."

He slammed the door behind him, but as she started to move into the other seat, he grasped her hips and pulled her into his lap and over his thighs while he slid to the right. He plopped her behind the wheel as he took the passenger seat.

She was having a little trouble breathing after that sensual slide over his hard thighs but she grasped the steering wheel and felt a shiver of delight go through her.

His soft chuckle pulled her attention to him. "You're really into this aren't you?"

She nodded.

"Have you driven a car like this before?"

She nodded again. "I've driven two Camaros and a Mustang Boss 429."

"No way."

She grinned at him. "Seriously."

"Those are rare."

"It was awesome."

He slowly shook his head, watching her. "Where's this all come from?"

She shook her head. "Doesn't matter."

"Oh, I think it does."

She could hear the amusement in his voice. "Nope." She reached for the ignition, but it was empty. She looked over at him. The keys were dangling from his index finger.

"You know," she said coyly—though she wasn't sure she'd

ever said anything coyly before in her life— "if I *don't* drive, you don't get whatever you want from me."

His eyes narrowed, as if he was assessing the situation. Then he reached over and stuck the key in the ignition. "Fine. But I will find out."

Annabelle felt a little thrill of power. She wasn't even sure what he wanted from her exactly, but it was a heady feeling thinking that he wanted it this much.

She fought the stupid grin that was threatening as she reached for the key. She cranked it and felt the car come to life. Zac Brown Band's *Whatever It Is* blasted from the speakers, adding to the noise around her. Oh, baby, that was good.

Her mother would be appalled.

With that thought, she pressed down on the gas and they shot out of the parking lot and onto the street.

Jackson gripped the dash. "Let's keep it on the pavement, okay Hotshot?" he said over the music.

She didn't look at him as she turned onto the highway. Her foot was itching to press harder and her heart was racing.

"Head for Cooper's Hill," Jackson said, settling back.

She glanced over at him. He was watching her with a grin. "What?" she asked, returning his smile.

"Hot," he said. "Very, very hot."

She liked that. She didn't think she'd ever been described as hot, but damn, behind the wheel of this car she felt it. She reluctantly turned the radio down. "Where's Cooper's Hill?"

He hesitated for a second. "You don't know?"

She looked over at him again. "No. Why?"

"It's the make-out spot from high school."

There were a number of interesting things in that sentence. "I've never been." But they were going now?

"You've never been to Cooper's Hill?"

She shook her head. She'd never made out with anyone in high school so that sort of made sense. "Sorry."

"Take a right at the baseball diamond, out past the cemetery six miles and a left."

She liked that idea. The paved road past the cemetery would have no traffic and she could push the speedometer.

Jackson chuckled when it happened and she grinned as she pushed it up to eighty.

"Girl, we've got a corner coming up," he cautioned.

She looked over. "Thought you were the wild one? You nervous?"

He raised an eyebrow. "Thought you were the good girl?"

"I don't even know where Cooper's Hill is."

"Ah, but you're about to."

There was something in his voice—that gravel again, or maybe the promise she heard under the words—that made her heart pick up as if she'd hit another ten miles per hour.

She did slow down in time to make the corner, with only a slight tire squeal and a tiny fishtail. Jackson didn't say anything but she could see him shaking his head out of the corner of her eye as he grabbed the dash again.

"Turn in up there." He pointed to a dirt drive. They bumped along the barely there trail for about a mile and then he pointed. "Right up there."

There was a grove of trees in the middle of what was basically a field. But she knew they didn't even have a mile before the ground would become marshy.

"This is where everyone came to make out?" she asked.

"And drink beer and smoke and cuss and listen to the music our parents hated."

She pulled up underneath a tree and killed the engine. It was dark and there wasn't much to see, but she suspected the same would be true even in daylight. It also wasn't really a hill. It was just a rise in the land before it started its descent to the swamplands and slow moving waters of the bayou.

Lit by the nearly full moon, it was peaceful, she'd give it that.

And it was away from town, making getting caught less of a chance. But dang, they were pretty far out here. If they'd been drinking, the drive home could have been dangerous.

"Did you guys have designated drivers?" she asked, looking from the silvery landscape to Jackson.

He was watching her, his bemused expression clear in the moonlight.

"So we have something in common, huh?"

Okay, they were going to dive right into that.

She chewed on the inside of her cheek for a moment, trying to figure out how to say it. Finally she said simply, "Everyone here has their minds made up about me."

Jackson nodded. "I can relate."

"I know." It was strange feeling a kinship with Jackson, of all people, but she did. And she suspected some of the not-completely-accurate labels had been assigned to him even before his troubled senior year.

But the truth remained that she could be good for his reputation.

And the converse could be true for *her* reputation.

"And they're not completely wrong about me," she said. "I do love my books, I love being at home, I have trouble feeling comfortable at parties and I have no idea how to talk to any of the men my age who live here."

Jackson seemed to be considering that. "You don't go for the type of guy who lives here, do you?"

She swallowed. "I tell myself that I want to date writers and academics, and I have. I like going out with them because I feel in control. I can keep up with any conversation about politics or literature or art. I can, pretty much, control the whole relationship. I know exactly how to handle those guys. But..." She trailed off.

Why was she telling him all of this? Holy crap, she hadn't even shared a lot of this with Randi or Regan or Priscilla.

"Oh, come on, you can't leave me hanging like that." Jackson shifted so his back was against the car door and he was fully facing her.

Fine. What the hell?

"It's like these cars." She ran her hand around the steering wheel again. "My VW bug gets me from point A to point B. It's fun and a little different and perfectly easy to handle. Seems right for me. But..." She sighed. "I don't get the thrill from her that I get in this car."

"So you want a guy who's a little hard to handle?" Jackson asked, that rumbly voice back.

Lord that voice did something to her, down deep.

She nodded. "I guess so. No matter how many nice guys I date, no matter how much we have in common, I feel this urge to...have...something else. More." She said the last word softly, not sure she should share that and amazed by how much one word could mean.

"More." It didn't sound like a question. He seemed as if he was pondering something very deep. "Seems to me that these other guys aren't interesting to you because they don't have anything to teach you, no way to challenge you. I can see why someone so similar to you wouldn't be enough. You get bored."

She stared at him. Then it hit her. Psych degree. Right.

"That...makes sense."

"You need a guy who looks at the world differently from you. Who has a different approach to life. Who's had different experiences and interests. Who can be more than what you already have and are used to."

She nodded.

"Like these cars. They're exciting to you because they're not anything you've experienced before. They make your heart beat faster because you're not absolutely sure what to expect and you feel something you're not used to feeling. It's just enough fear to be exciting."

Fear. She never would have used that word herself, but that was what it felt like. It was how she felt when she was in social situations and didn't know what to expect or when she was out of an environment she knew, like her classroom or meetings where she was in charge, or her home.

Fear.

And a rush of adrenaline that made her feel jittery and restless and…alive.

Jackson was watching her carefully.

"And you want a guy who will make you feel that way."

Her eyes widened. Yep, she would like a guy who would make her feel that way. Not fearful, but out of her element, able to let go. And alive.

"You think so?" she asked, trying for nonchalant.

He nodded slowly. "Like with the car," he said. "When you're driving this car you have to let it loose. You have to let go a little. And you love that rush. But you also need an excuse—more power than you're used to, touchy gas pedal, you've never driven one exactly like this before—whatever it is that gives you a reason to let go."

She didn't remember where he went to college, but their psych program was good.

"And you think it would be the same with men?" she asked.

Was that her voice that was so breathless?

He leaned away from the door. "I do. I think you've been waiting for a guy to come along who will take charge. Who will demand you give control to him. Someone who's not intimidated by you and the fact that you're not like any of the other women. Someone who will ensure that you have all the pleasure you need. Who will challenge you and show you new things about yourself and relationships and sex."

She was panting.

She couldn't believe it.

He was talking, hypothetically, about things she might need

from *someone* at *some point* and she was staring at him and panting.

"And there are guys around here like that?" she asked. The guys around here were different from what she was used to, that was for sure. But did they have...*that*? That delicious concoction Jackson had mentioned?

"There are guys around here like that," he said slowly. "Is there someone in particular you're curious about?"

"Michael."

Blurting his name out like that seemed immediately like a bad idea. Jackson's frown was instantaneous.

"LeClaire?"

She nodded. "I've had a little thing for him for a while."

Jackson pulled in a deep breath, obviously taken back. "Michael LeClaire is not the answer I was expecting," he said, as if he was choosing his words carefully.

"Why?"

"LeClaire comes to Bad specifically to *not* get serious. He comes here to blow off steam. His hometown is...tight. He's close to almost everyone there. He has a kid."

She nodded. "I know."

"So, he's not going to be...romancing anyone over here."

She wasn't sure what Jackson was getting at, exactly. It seemed he was trying to warn her about something. "Well, he isn't exactly begging me to go out with him."

"But you want him to." Jackson sounded irritated by that.

"He's good-looking, smart, funny, charming, wears a uniform—"

"Right. Got it. You sure you're ready for a guy who just wants to...let loose?"

Later, Annabelle planned to blame this on the feeling of confidence and what-the-hell the GTO gave her. She leaned in and said, "You're the one I kissed and left the bar with. I'm afraid you're going to have to show me letting loose first."

Even in the dark car, with the moon the only illumination,

Annabelle could see Jackson's eyes heat. Or maybe it was that the interior of the car heated by about twenty degrees all of a sudden.

When he finally spoke, his voice was rough and low. "You really want that?"

"I do." She answered without hesitation and she knew Jackson took note.

"Then you need to come over here."

A hot tingle started at her scalp and danced down her body to her toes.

Jackson shifted in his seat to face forward again and he reached down beside him for the lever that would allow him to slide the seat all the way back.

Which he did.

Making room.

Yep, she wanted to do this. If nothing else, because she'd been turned on by muscle cars for years but had never made out in one and that seemed a travesty.

But also because she couldn't think of anywhere she'd rather be than Jackson's lap.

She kicked off her boots and then gathered her skirt to climb over the middle console. She swung a leg over his thighs and he caught her calf in one big palm, his hand sliding up to the back of her knee and helping guide her leg.

Good thing. With his hand on her bare leg she forgot what she'd been in the middle of doing. When she froze, his hands went to her butt and he lifted her, finishing what she'd started—positioning her so she was straddling him.

Having his big hands on her butt was one thing. The fact that the one that had been on her leg had slid up *under* her skirt to get to her butt was another.

"Damn, I really do like these skirts," Jackson muttered, almost to himself.

He caressed the cheek he held, her panties the only thing between them. And that wasn't much. She felt every stroke and the heat spread from there through her whole body in about five seconds.

Annabelle braced her hands on his chest and waited. He'd said she needed a take-charge guy.

She was pretty sure she was face-to-face with him right now.

CHAPTER
SIX

HOLY SHIT.

There weren't better words.

Jackson couldn't believe what was happening. He'd come to town a week ago, thinking he'd be doing ranch work, helping Coach, maybe drinking some beer with the guys.

Now he sat at Cooper's Hill in his GTO with his lap and hands full, literally, of hot, sweet, willing woman. Not that the woman-on-his-lap thing was impossible to believe but that the hot, sweet, willing woman was Annabelle Hartington was a little crazy.

And he wasn't sure which of those words was the biggest surprise—hot, sweet or willing.

They had, however, established that she needed a take-charge guy to show her some new things and challenge her. He was muddled about how exactly they'd gotten on the subject. It had to do with his car. That was the bottom line for him. He'd never gone out with a woman who was as enamored with his car as Annabelle was.

The nerdy bookworm from high school who had turned into a beautiful bookworm as an adult had been on his mind enough.

Once he knew she had a thing for muscle cars, he wouldn't have been able to leave her alone anyway.

But now that he knew she needed, and wanted, some dominating—yeah, he was the guy and it was starting right now.

"So us non-professor types like to get bossy and talk dirty, that okay with you?" he asked.

He knew lots of non-professor types, but he liked to think he was more evolved now than to assume the men here were all alike. Still, he absolutely knew some guys in Bad who were a lot like him and did, for sure, like to get bossy and talk dirty.

Michael LeClaire wasn't a Bad boy but he fit right in in a lot of ways. That was one. He knew from the guys—and some of the girls—that LeClaire came over to party and have fun away from his friends and family in Autre where he felt he had to be more responsible.

If Annabelle was looking for a boyfriend, Jackson didn't think Michael was the guy.

Which saved Jackson from having to punch LeClaire in the face. There was something about the thought of Annabelle hooking up with Michael that made Jackson a little irrational. He wasn't going to try to analyze that. *Not* analyzing himself was a very good idea most of the time.

But of all the guys in the area, Annabelle had to want LeClaire? Sure, Michael didn't show any signs of wanting to settle down, but if he did…he'd be great for Annabelle. He was a hell of a guy. He was a dad, for fuck's sake. By all accounts, his kid was awesome. Jackson knew Michael was also widely respected as a fire chief, EMT, and just general good guy who loved his community and family.

Dammit.

"I think I can handle bossy and talking dirty," she said.

He loved that breathless voice she used. And the fact that it was real. She wasn't doing it to be flirtatious. She was doing it because he made her breathless.

Yep, he liked that a lot.

"This is how this goes," he said, digging for his demanding side.

It wasn't real deep, but it was out of practice. He used a much more cooperative approach with the kids he worked with, and yes, with the women he dated. He liked his congenial, laid-back side. Maintaining that side was more of a challenge, and that he was able to do it was a true accomplishment. Being demanding was a piece of cake.

"I tell you what to do and you do it. It takes trust and it takes letting go of the little voices in your head that tell you all the reasons *not* to," he said, squeezing the firm curve of her ass. "Since it might be a little early for you to completely trust me, it's going to take even more to let go. But if you like the rush of driving a sixty-nine GTO, I promise you that this rush is even better."

Her eyes widened but she was looking at him with interest, not worry.

He was *helping* her. He was going to keep telling himself that. If Annabelle wanted to mess with LeClaire—or any of the Bad boys—she needed some coaching.

"Do we need a safe word?" she asked.

His whole body hardened instantly. Damn if the idea of pushing Annabelle like that didn't stir his blood.

"We don't need a safe word," he told her gruffly. "No is fine. If you say no, we stop."

It was a pretty big leap from the front seat of his GTO to role-playing some kinky captive-captor fantasy where no didn't actually mean stop. Of course, it was a pretty big leap from where they'd been ten years ago to the front seat of his GTO. Yet here they were, with her skirt hiked up and his hand on her panties.

"Just no," he repeated, reminding himself as well. "We'll... reassess as we go."

She squirmed on his lap and Jackson groaned. That was enough right there. He didn't need to role-play with this woman, he didn't need to tie her up, he didn't need any toys. She was a real-life fantasy—the innocent librarian type wanting to tangle with the bad boy.

And oh were they going to tangle.

"Okay," she said, nodding. "Otherwise, I do what you say."

He nodded, consciously having to work to keep his hands from gripping her too hard and his next words from being something like "take your panties off and bend over the hood of the car".

"And enjoy, Annabelle," he said huskily. "Do what I say and enjoy."

Her gaze went to his mouth and Jackson bit back another groan.

"What if I want more of something?" she asked. "Can I say that?"

Damn. Annabelle Hartington was going to be a good time.

He shook his head. "I'm in charge. I'll be able to tell if you like something."

"But if I like something, you'll keep doing it?"

She was eager. He really liked that.

"If I want to," he said. "But if I think it's better to make you wait for it, I'll do that. If I decide to make you beg for it, I'll do that. I'm in charge."

He wasn't typically a demanding asshole in bed. Or anywhere else. At least, he worked to not be. Sometimes it turned a woman on for him to get dominant, but for the most part those women would simply say "tie me up and fuck me" and he'd oblige.

He, like Annabelle, dated people he had a lot in common with—women who were confident, experienced, as willing to get on top and take over as to want him to.

But he couldn't deny that being in charge, having a woman like Annabelle *let* him be in charge, spoke to a primal part of him. The part of him that wanted to be trusted like that.

"I haven't said no yet," she said softly.

He was sitting there staring at her, his mind reeling.

She had no idea how hard he was trying to be good. He wanted to push her and test her. She had no idea that she was playing right into the fantasies that stirred him the most—where he was given absolute control and trust. She had no idea what trusting him could mean.

But she hadn't said no… *yet*.

Fine. Either she was going to go with it, or she wasn't.

"Let's go over where we're starting from," he said, sounding much more controlled than he felt. "You're not a virgin?"

She bit her lower lip and Jackson had to hold back a groan. She shook her head.

"How many guys?"

"Two," she almost whispered.

Two. Holy crap. He wondered if he'd ever been with a woman who'd had only two other partners. Not since high school, he was almost certain.

"Do you have a vibrator?"

Even in the dim light he could see her blush. Her cheeks practically glowed. She nodded slowly.

Jackson's imagination exploded with images. He had to clear his throat and force himself to focus. They'd get there. Definitely. But they could work up to that. Not that he expected this to be a long, drawn-out seduction. That wasn't the purpose here. Annabelle could find herself a nice small-town boy for that. She wanted Jackson to show her the wild side to the guys in Bad.

But she wanted LeClaire.

A nice small-town boy.

Not that LeClaire didn't have a hell of a lot of fun, but if anyone was going to be a long, drawn-out seduction guy, he'd put money on LeClaire.

Fuck.

Focus, Brady. That's not what you're here for.

Though his hand was quite comfortable on her ass, Jackson stroked his palm down her hip and outer thigh. Her skin was silky smooth and hot. He couldn't wait to get his lips on it.

"How about oral sex?" he asked. "You ever let a guy do that to you?"

She bit her lip again and hesitated. Jackson felt his body winding tighter as he waited for her answer.

"Annabelle? You gotta tell me what I'm working with here."

God, he hoped she'd never had a guy's mouth on her sweet pussy. He'd love to be that guy, the first to show her how fan-fucking-tastic that could be.

"You ever had a guy's tongue inside you?" he asked, pushing her with his words only. For now. "You ever had a guy suck on your clit? You ever have a guy get you off with his mouth and fingers only?"

She was panting, staring at him unblinking, the air between them hot and thick.

"No." Her head moved back and forth slowly, her eyes on his.

He respected that. She might be embarrassed. Lord knew he'd never expected to have this conversation with Annabelle Hartington. He was sure the possibility of telling him the details of her sex life had never occurred to her either. But she wasn't hiding, she wasn't pulling back, she wasn't running or pushing him away or saying no.

He fucking loved that.

There was something about knowing she was giving him private details that made him even more determined to increase that intimacy.

"How about blow jobs?" he asked. His hand slid back up to her butt and this time slipped between her skin and the silk panties. Skin to skin, he brought her forward on his lap. "You ever sucked a guy's cock?" he asked hoarsely.

She sucked in a quick breath, but this time she nodded. "Once."

Damn. Not that it did a single thing to make him *not* ache with the need to have his cock sliding past the lip that she would not stop biting. Still, there were apparently a few things he could teach her.

"But I didn't want to," she added.

He stilled and looked from her mouth to her eyes. "What's that mean? He forced you?" A new tightness wound through Jackson's body. Hot sex, pushing boundaries, even some not-so-sweet stuff was great if *both* people were into it. Making a woman do something she didn't want to was unacceptable. If someone had—

"No, I agreed to it," she said. "I just didn't *want* to do it. It was fine."

Jackson pulled a breath in through his nose then let it out slowly. "You don't—"

"But with you, I already want to. We've only kissed and I really, really want to…"

She trailed off and Jackson sorted his thoughts quickly. She hadn't wanted to give a blow job to whoever-he-was but she wanted to give Jackson one.

He could work with that. And be eternally grateful.

"Say it," he commanded softly. "Tell me what you really, really want to do."

She bit her lip again.

He almost chuckled. "You have to get used to talking this way, Hotshot."

She didn't. People could have sex—good sex—without the talk. There were probably millions of women who had never ever said the word "cock" and still had great sex.

But he wanted Annabelle to say it. To him. About him.

She swallowed hard. "What do you want me to say?"

"Tell me you want to suck my cock."

Her thighs tightened on his and he wondered if she knew she was giving her arousal away. She might not be used to the words, but they affected her.

It would probably kill him to hear it out loud, but it wasn't only the words he wanted, it was knowing he could get

Annabelle to step outside of her comfort zone. And this was just the start.

She pressed her lips together, studying his face. Several seconds passed before she finally leaned in. But she didn't whisper the words in his ear. Instead, she took his face in her hands and pressed her lips to his.

Her palms cradled his jaw, her mouth moving over his softly. One of his hands came up to cup the back of her head. He let her lead at first. He loved the hunger he sensed behind the surface hesitation. It was as though she wanted to make it hotter, like she wanted to dive in, but was holding back. Testing him.

And maybe she was. And maybe he was going to fail spectacularly. But he couldn't resist.

He brought her up against his erection, opened his mouth and took over.

His tongue thrust against hers, his hand on her ass pressed her against his rock-hard cock, and he took her hair in his other fist with just enough force that she knew he was in charge.

She moaned against his mouth and her arms went around his neck, pressing her breasts into his chest. And damn if she didn't grind her hips against his.

Jackson drank in the sound and feel of her acquiescence.

Making out with a woman like Annabelle and realizing she was going to give him everything he wanted was like giving a shot of whiskey to an alcoholic. There would be no turning back until he'd been totally consumed, done some really stupid things and was lying on the floor wrecked.

He pulled back, still holding her head, and stared up at her.

He should warn her. Or something. "Annabelle—"

"I want to suck your cock."

Heat, hunger, lust, and yes, gratitude, slammed into him. He hadn't indulged in a fling with a good girl in forever. He stayed away from good girls. He always fucked things up outside of the bedroom as good as he did inside of it. But this had been her idea. Annabelle knew he was a screw-up deep down and couldn't be trusted long-term with serious things. So this would be fine. She could trust him for the hot sex and the bad reputation she seemed to want. No question.

"Take your top off."

Her eyes widened but she didn't hesitate or question him. That was very good.

She stripped the shirt off and tossed it into the driver's seat. She wore a simple bra. White, with a little bit of lace over the top of the cups. There was nothing particularly sexy about it. Except that her nipples were hard and clearly defined behind the satin. Somehow those hard tips straining against the simple nothing-special bra, straining for *him*, made him hotter than any lingerie ever had. She hadn't planned this. This was no seduction. She hadn't worn this to make him crazy. And that made him crazier than anything else could have.

His gaze didn't waver. "Take it off."

She knew what he meant because her hands went behind her back, the slight arch to her spine pushed her breasts forward. She wasn't big. She was more on the petite side. But his mouth watered.

The bra fell away a moment later and Annabelle sat in his lap, naked from the waist up.

He took in the full sight. Her hair was messed up from his hand, her lips swollen from his kisses. Her eyes were bright and wide with anticipation and her cheeks flushed with arousal. And her nipples, her gorgeous, perfect, I-could-spend-a-week-on-them-alone nipples, were hard and pink and all for him.

"Play with them," he ordered.

He wanted to play with them. Pinch them, suck them, feel them against his chest, watch them bounce as he fucked her. But first…

She lifted her hands to her breasts, cupping them.

"Show me what you like," he told her.

She'd like whatever he did to her. She probably didn't even

know what all she liked. But he needed to see what she would do with his commands.

Annabelle ran her thumbs over the tips, back and forth, her lips falling open as she breathed. Then she slid her hands so her nipples were between her first two fingers. She squeezed her fingers together.

Again her thighs tightened on either side of his.

He looked up at her. Her eyes were locked on his.

"Harder."

She caught her breath. It was so soft, he wouldn't have noticed if he hadn't been looking for it.

Then his gaze was drawn back to her breasts as she took her nipples between her thumbs and fingers and tugged.

Damn, that was hot.

He opened his mouth to give her further commands, but she began alternatingly rolling and tugging and rubbing, and thought fled.

Watching her work her breasts made him absolutely certain he wanted to see her working other parts of her just as hard. He could put her back in the driver's seat, one heel propped on the dashboard and one on the back of the seat with her skirt bunched at her waist. Or he could spread her out on the hood of the car. That way, once she'd made herself come, he could take a long, satisfying taste of her—

She shifted up onto her knees, putting a nipple right in front of his mouth.

Or they could do this.

His hands splayed on her upper back, he leaned in and captured the hard tip between his lips. He licked and sucked, making her writhe against him. His hands held her still for his ministrations. Then he bit gently.

"*Jackson.*" Her hands went into his hair.

He waited to feel her pulling him away, but instead she shifted so her other breast was at his mouth. He feasted on that side as well, her sounds—soft whimpers of need—encouraging him.

"Oh...I... Please..."

God, he loved making women beg. He wondered how often and for what Annabelle had begged before this.

"More. Please."

Yes, more. That was exactly what they both needed.

He pulled back, letting her nipple go reluctantly. The ripe tip glistened in the moonlight from his mouth. He liked things that glistened. He had to give it one more lick.

She gasped, her fingers tightening on his shoulders.

"Put your hand in your panties," he told her.

She hesitated. A flash of vulnerability lit her eyes and Jackson literally bit his tongue. She wasn't sure. He got that. Completely. This was crazy and fast and they were the last two people on earth he ever would have considered together. But he wasn't stopping. She had to know that. *She* could stop it. She would have to be the one and of course he'd let her.

But he wasn't going to be a good guy here.

He caught the irony. He was going to pretend to date Annabelle so the rest of the town would think he *was* a good guy. No, he corrected himself, so they would *know* he was a good guy. He'd grown up, changed, gotten his shit together. But in the front seat of his GTO with a half-naked woman was a whole different story.

Annabelle moved her hand up under her skirt.

She was going to do it.

"Touch yourself."

And damn if she didn't keep her eyes locked on his. In the dark, with her skirt in the way, he couldn't see what she was doing but he could see it in her face when she brushed over her clit. She blew out a soft breath, then licked her lips.

"Now slide your fingers inside." He was barely restraining himself as her hand moved. "Two of them. Nice and deep." Not being able to see what she was doing made it even hotter. She made a little sound, not quite a moan, not quite a gasp, but tempting. So damn tempting. "Are you wet?" he asked huskily.

"Yes," she whispered.

"Your fingers are wet?"

"Yes."

"I want to taste you."

He couldn't wait. He wanted his tongue on her five minutes ago. She still had that no to use if she needed it.

She shifted, her hand slipping out from underneath the skirt.

He was going to have to lay the seat back or they were going to have to climb into the backseat for him to get his mouth where he wanted it. Jackson started to reach for the lever on the side of the seat when Annabelle lifted her fingers to his mouth.

He stared at her. *Holy…*

That wasn't what he'd meant but that would *totally* work.

He only hesitated with surprise for a heartbeat but she sensed it. He felt her stiffen and start to pull back. He grabbed her wrist and slid her fingers into his mouth.

Her pupils dilated and she swallowed hard. Jackson kept his eyes on hers as he ran his tongue up and down the length of her fingers. She tasted so fucking good. He sucked lightly, then at her gasp, harder. She was squirming on his lap after only a few seconds.

"Jackson."

He kept hold of her wrist, but slid her fingers out of his mouth sensually. "Take your panties off and bend over the hood of the car."

He'd known he was going to use that line on her eventually. Probably the moment she'd run her hand over the hood as if she'd never seen something so beautiful.

"The hood? Now?" But she wasn't scandalized. She sounded eager.

He grinned at her. "Thank God you're not wearing jeans with bling all over. That might scratch her up. One more reason to love these skirts."

"Have you... scratched the paint before?"

Her question really was "have you fucked another woman on the hood of this car?" and to that he could happily answer, "Never."

Annabelle looked downright naughty as she reached for the door handle. She had the door swung open and had shifted to get out when he grasped her hips, stalling her.

"Annabelle."

She looked at him. "Yeah?"

"If you get out and bend over the hood, I'm going to lick you to orgasm and then take you from behind."

She needed to know. He needed to know that she knew. As far as he was concerned, it had been pretty clear where they were going but she was a lot less experienced. It was important they were absolutely clear—

"You'd better," she said simply, sliding off his lap and onto the soft grass.

Her eyes on his, she reached under her skirt and proceeded to wiggle her way out of her panties. She tossed them into the driver's seat and then gave him a little smile before she turned and sashayed her pretty butt to the front of the car.

CHAPTER
SEVEN

JACKSON COULDN'T MAKE his brain and body connect. Well, he couldn't connect with any part of his body other than the huge, throbbing erection Annabelle had left behind.

He gave a little growl and got out, stalking toward her. She was leaning with her butt against the car, her hands braced on the hood on either side of her hips, bare breasted, a sly, purely feminine-power grin on her face.

Oh, she thought she had him wrapped around her finger now?

Fine. She could think that. The entire time she was spread out and begging him for release.

"Turn around," he said firmly.

Her eyes widened, but she spun to face the car.

"Hands on the hood. Don't move them," he ordered.

She did exactly as she was told.

"Lean over."

He moved in behind her. Her hair hung over her back and he ran a strand between his fingers, then he brushed the mass over one of her shoulders, exposing the smooth skin of her back. He ran his index finger up and down the gentle curve of her spine. Goose bumps broke out in the wake of his touch and she shivered. That probably made her nipples harder. He reached around and cupped one breast in his hand, the tip pressing between his two middle and ring fingers. He squeezed gently as he massaged her butt cheek through the skirt with his other hand.

The night was warm, only a slight breeze stirred the air. The soft grass under their feet was long enough to brush against their calves. It was dark, moonlight and stars the only things breaking up the deep black sky. It was all decadent.

The chances of being caught were practically nonexistent. But it wasn't impossible.

Jackson wondered how Annabelle would respond to that reminder.

"Once I've got my mouth and hands and cock in your pussy, I'm not stopping," he said in a growl near her ear. "If someone drives in, they're going to get to watch me fucking you, get to hear you cry out when you come harder than you ever have."

She moaned, her head dropping forward, her butt pressing into his hand.

He grinned. Good response. Very good response.

She liked the word fuck. And fucking. And fucked. And cock. And pussy.

She liked the dirty talk. Very good to know. The graphic talk was natural for him, but he could hold back if needed. Still he was thrilled Annabelle responded to it. This was only one of the things about her the other guys wouldn't believe.

Jackson frowned at that. He didn't want to tell anyone else. He loved knowing this side of her and it felt like something he wanted to keep to himself. Something that was almost too intimate to share. As if she'd trusted him with a secret.

But she wanted him to tell the other guys. The idea of them dating had been to get the guys in Bad to look at her differently.

And the fact that Annabelle Hartington had a naughty streak and loved the word cock would be welcome news. He was sure the men did see her as uptight and unapproachable, but she was beautiful and sweet and smart and funny and had layers that were fascinating and could keep a guy interested for…ever. To find out that the good girl had a sinful side would be like finding buried treasure in your backyard—it had always been there just waiting to be discovered.

Jackson dropped to his knees behind her. He had found the treasure first. He was going to claim at least part of it.

"Spread your legs, Annabelle," he said, gathering her skirt and pushing it up over her hips. Her position—bent over and leaning on the hood—kept it in place.

She moved her feet farther apart.

"Oh, this is pretty," he praised. The submissive position was part of it. The wickedness of bunching her skirt at her waist was part of it. But everything from her dainty ankles to the gorgeous curve of her ass, offered up in the night air to his eyes and hands… he was a very happy man.

Then there was the shadow between her legs.

He did curse the lack of light as he knelt behind her. He wanted to see every gorgeous pink inch of her.

But when presented with the lack of sight, you had to make up for it with other senses.

Touch was his favorite of the senses, followed quickly by taste.

He ran his hands up her legs from ankle to ass. Over and over. Each time his hands went higher, slowly worked toward the inner thighs, his thumbs coming closer and closer to her hot, wet center.

Finally his thumbs met and brushed over hot, wet woman.

She groaned.

So did he.

He repeated the motion, dragging his thumbs slower over the shadowed area where he wanted to spend the next couple of days—straight.

He met her clit with the pads of his thumbs, then dragged back, over her wet cleft. He slipped one into the silky heat to the first knuckle. She whimpered and pressed back as if seeking more.

Jackson was thrilled that she'd assumed the position, but was surprised she was maintaining it.

He slipped his other thumb in as well, filling her.

She moved harder against him, clearly wanting more. So he slid them both in farther, together.

Annabelle bent over, folding her arms on the hood and dropping her head onto them as if she could no longer stay upright.

He liked that. He slid his thumbs in and out, then switched to his two middle fingers, pumping them deep. She was wet and hot and writhing.

So he grasped her hips and put his tongue where his thumbs had been. He started with one long lick. She was delicious, as was the little squeal she gave.

"Damn, I could do this all day," he told her. He licked again and again. Then found her clit and flicked his tongue quickly over the sweet nub.

She cried out and Jackson wanted lots more. He shifted so that he was underneath her and had more direct pressure on her clit. She was now straddling his face and when he circled her clit, slid two fingers into her, then sucked—hard—she pressed against his mouth.

The only problem with all of this—and there truly was only one problem—was that there were no mirrors, so Jackson couldn't watch the gorgeous scene at the same time he was participating.

He did like mirrors.

"Jackson!" She gasped and he felt her inner muscles tightening around his fingers.

"Come for me," he urged. He licked, thrust and sucked and within a minute she clamped onto his fingers, let out a heartfelt "oh my God" and came.

He didn't even let the ripples fade. He moved quickly,

moving to stand behind her, unzipping, donning a condom. He lifted her, turning her to sit on the edge of the car.

"Damn, you're gorgeous," he told her. "Lay back and open up."

She did. Her hair spilled around her, pale swirls on the top of his dark car. She opened her legs and he was thankful to his bones for the bright moonlight. In this position he could see much better.

She seemed to be without even a flicker of doubt or self-consciousness. She let him look, then she let him drag his finger up and down through the slick sweetness he'd helped create, then she met his gaze when he stepped in, his cock so hard, so ready for her, he feared he'd only last two or three strokes.

"This car was built for hard and fast," she said. "Even when it's parked."

He stopped, stared at her, then grinned. "Even when it's parked," he repeated under his breath. "Damn right."

He cupped her ass in his hands and brought her closer.

Hard and fast indeed. Just looking at her like this was almost enough to send him over the edge.

He moved his hips and thrust, burying himself deep in her tight, wet heat.

"God, Annabelle," he groaned. He moved slowly at first, enjoying the friction and the way she moved and sounded and looked.

Deep. Deeper than it had ever felt before. And hot. So hot.

But slow didn't last long. Hard and fast became the mantra and Jackson felt her climax building again.

Oh yeah. He could do this pretty much every night for the rest of his life.

That stray thought gave him a quick burst of what-the-fuck-is-that, but then her hot, sweet body began milking him and all he could do was thrust and groan as his orgasm coiled tighter and tighter.

Finally Annabelle clamped down on him, her back arched

and she cried out his name.

Jackson let loose. He thrust harder, pounding into her, until his orgasm ripped through him from deep in his gut.

It took several long, deep-breathing seconds before Jackson could move. He'd braced his hands on either side of her on the car and dropped his head, bringing in much needed oxygen.

Holy shit.

He wondered if he'd ever stop thinking that when it came to her.

This was *Annabelle* and he'd just had some of the best sex of his life.

Finally she stirred under him and he pulled back.

She pushed her hair away from her face and looked up at him, her eyes filled with a combination of things, including wonder—which he liked, a lot—and confusion and a hint of trepidation.

Oh no, she was not going to regret this.

He caught her chin in his hand. "Hey," he said softly.

"Hey."

"You're amazing."

She gave him a small smile. "That was...unusual for me."

"Good." He knew she could hear the sincerity in his voice.

And the fact that he meant it startled him too. He was used to women who knew what they wanted. They might let him be in charge, be demanding, but they did it because they knew they wanted it. He was pretty sure Annabelle had had no idea what this would do to her.

He fucking loved it.

"I think we need to do a lot more of that," he told her, not letting her break eye contact.

She took a deep breath and blew it out, the air warm against his cheek. "Thank goodness."

He stared at her for a minute, then laughed. "You thought I might not want to?" he asked in disbelief.

She shrugged. "This isn't new for you."

But it was. It hit him as she said it. This felt...very new.

Of course it was way too soon, way too crazy to *say* that out loud to her, so he said, "It was fucking incredible and if you'll let me, I will make that body of yours sing over and over again."

A little shiver went through her and he couldn't hold back his cocky grin.

"I think I could be okay with that."

She was going to be a lot better than okay. He kissed her, slow and sweet and hot, then stepped back and they both got as cleaned up as they could in a field, got dressed and got back into the car.

Annabelle slid behind the wheel.

"You're driving again?" he asked, leaning on the top of the car, caging her in.

She was at eye level with his stomach and her eyes roamed south, then slowly back up his torso to finally meet his gaze.

He was ready for her again just like that.

She gave him an impish smile. "I think I'm going to be driving your car a lot."

He reached in and tugged on a strand of her hair. The hair that was loose and wild because of him and his hands and the night breeze and the way she'd been writhing and squirming on the hood of his car. "You did all of that so you could keep driving my car, huh?"

She laughed and turned the key. "This is what's called icing on the cake."

The motion of her hand starting the car drew his attention to the small tattoo on the inside of her wrist. Damn, he'd gotten so caught up he hadn't even remembered to search for the other tattoos.

He was going to have to correct that oversight. Soon.

He got in on the passenger side, feeling something that went way beyond physical, sexual satisfaction. This was going to be fun.

· · ·

"I love yoga days," Jackson said three days later as Annabelle approached where he stood outside of Bad Habit.

He held out a cup. Made exactly right, almost as if he'd paid attention that first day or had asked about it. His hot gaze swept over her and she felt her cheeks flush.

She was more aware of her body over the past three days than she had been in her entire life. Not just because of the way Jackson looked at her whenever they were together—skirts or yoga pants—but because of sore muscles that had never been sore before and parts of her that tingled that had never tingled before.

She didn't do yoga every morning, but when he watched her walking toward him, looking as if he was starving and she was a large pizza with everything on it, she wanted to wear those pants every day. The last two mornings she'd been wearing her typical skirts, on her way to meet with a couple of her students who were running a summer literacy program.

She took the cup from him, her hand sliding across his completely on purpose.

It had been two nights since the car and she wanted more. A lot more. Right now.

She'd seen him and talked to him. He'd met her outside the coffee shop the morning after he'd left her at her car at Bad Brews, sated and grinning. And now it had already become a habit to find him standing on the sidewalk with two cups when she got there each morning.

She hadn't really stopped grinning since.

They'd seen each other somewhat regularly but it wasn't enough. Which should bother her. She couldn't get attached to him. This was temporary. This was for the benefit of other people in town. They were helping each other out. Friends.

But that word felt weird. They were friends? How had that happened? Surely not. They'd had sex and coffee. That wasn't any kind of relationship at all.

Still, when she saw him leaning against the coffee shop with her coffee, she felt her heart flip a little.

He was so good-looking for one thing. He was dressed in a pair of faded blue jeans that looked soft from repeated washings and molded to his body—the muscular thighs and tight ass and impressive other things—as if he'd been wearing them for years. He wore work boots and a dark-blue T-shirt stretched over his wide, hard chest. She knew he'd just come from the ranch. That was also tempting. She didn't typically go for guys who worked with their hands, who sweated and got dirty, but she wanted to run her hands over his shoulders, abs…lower.

She was horny.

That had to be it.

Looking at his hand curled around the paper cup made her think about that hand on her breast, between her legs, holding the back of her head as he kissed her.

Watching him drink from the cup made her think about his lips on hers, on her breast, between her legs and the dirty things he said. She got hot even thinking about it.

She had never considered herself a woman who would like a take-charge guy like that but…she so did.

She wanted to have sex again.

They hadn't done more than have coffee and text a few times during the day. The texting had surprised her. The dating was supposed to be for everyone else to see. What did texting have to do with it? No one would know about it but her. Unless she told her friends. Maybe that was the plan. He'd texted things like "how's your day?" and "you looked beautiful this morning", along with things like "I swear I can still taste you on my tongue" and "I can't stop thinking about how hot and wet and tight you were."

She'd go hot and flushed and she was sure people noticed. Randi had even commented on it at one point, asking if she was feeling sick.

They hadn't had sex again though and Annabelle was feeling itchy. She'd had dinner with her parents one night, Jackson had been working on the ranch 'til late another night doing something with a cow that she didn't understand—and didn't want to understand. Plus, she supposed having him come over after midnight and keep her up until the wee hours wasn't conducive to their plan. People had to see them together. Or at least notice Jackson's car in her driveway. Her neighborhood was nice and quiet and everyone was in bed and fast asleep right after the nightly news. Jackson could come over, make her sore and tingly and be gone before any of them were up for their morning coffee.

Which wouldn't forward their plan at all. She had to remember that.

She'd been stuck taking care of the tingles on her own the last two nights.

They turned and started walking toward the yoga studio. "How about dinner at my place next week?" she asked. "You've helped me out with my side of things. I need to step up."

Jackson didn't say anything to that at first and she looked up at him. "I thought I'd invite a bunch of people. Maybe Jase and Priscilla could come. And I thought I'd include a couple of people from the school board. Sally MacDonald will be board president next year and her husband Troy is a huge football fan. They're very nice people. I thought maybe Daisy would be a good addition since she's a friend and has kids in school. I also thought Michael might be a good idea. He gets a long well with Jase and Troy is the fire chief here, so they obviously know each other well. That makes the whole group a little more casual and gives everyone common ground and stuff to talk about."

She figured they needed some friends to help make the dinner more casual and relaxed and less like a job interview for Jackson.

Jackson kept walking, not speaking, but she felt a tension emanating from him all of a sudden.

"Just so it doesn't seem like I'm setting up an impromptu

interview," she said. "I don't want to invite only school board members or only members of the search committee. I should include people who would typically come to a dinner party at my house."

He still said nothing.

"Or we could go to dinner downtown," she finally said. "If you don't want to come over. We should probably start being seen out together for more than coffee."

Finally he stopped walking and turned to face her. "I'd love to have dinner with you. And I appreciate you setting up a dinner party to help me out."

She looked into his eyes, trying to decipher what he was thinking or feeling. Nothing was clear. "You're sure?"

"Of course. We want people to know we're dating. That seems perfect, actually."

There was something weird in his tone but she couldn't tell what it was. Because she didn't know him that well. She needed to remember that. It was strange that she had to keep reminding herself of it though.

"Then next Thursday night at my house. Do you like pasta?"

"I like pasta," he said simply.

Great. Lasagna it was.

He'd said yes. She was going to do her part to make their deal work. Why did she feel as though something was wrong? But they weren't close enough to delve into things like that. They were doing each other a favor. She just needed to do it.

They turned and continued down the sidewalk. "I'll be on the ranch all day today," Jackson commented.

"I've got yoga and then I'm helping Mrs. Simons paint her kitchen."

He looked over at her and when Annabelle looked up, she found him smiling at her. The tension in her shoulders let go and she returned the smile.

"You really are a nice girl, aren't you?" he asked.

Everyone knew Jacqueline Simons. She'd been a staple in the

community for years. She'd run a local craft store forever. She'd also done daycare, did sewing and quilting for people, taught music lessons and attended every single sporting event in Bad. She'd been one of the biggest boosters for the football team.

Annabelle shrugged. "She taught me piano lessons from the time I was six until I graduated. She's like a grandmother to me."

"That wouldn't matter. She could be a total stranger and you'd still be helping her paint her kitchen."

He said it matter-of-factly and it made Annabelle smile. For the most part, she liked being considered a nice girl. Who wouldn't? It was better than many things people could think or say about her. Other than the fact that the guys in Bad apparently steered clear of good girls, she didn't mind people thinking she was kind and sweet.

Of course, she now knew what she'd been missing in the sex-with-a-bad-boy department and she thought she'd be willing to give up almost anything to get more of that.

She bit her tongue though. She couldn't *ask* Jackson for more sex. Could she?

"Have a great class," he said, stopping.

Annabelle realized they were in front of the yoga studio. "Oh. Right. Thanks."

He leaned in and kissed her on the cheek. "See you later."

He gave her a wink and then headed back down the sidewalk.

Annabelle put her hand to her cheek and watched him go. When he'd rounded the corner at the end of the block, she turned toward the studio with a sigh. Several people inside the studio were watching her through the big picture window. They'd seen them together, seen the kiss.

Right. Kiss on the cheek. Because they were dating and Jackson was now a reformed bad boy and she was a nice girl and they would only have coffee and kiss on the cheek.

Right.

CHAPTER
EIGHT

SUNDAY EVENING, Jackson walked into Bad Brews. He'd put in several long, hot hours on the ranch over the last couple of days and knew he should be feeling more relaxed from it. He loved the hard work, the hot sun, the fatigue and ache in his muscles that said he'd accomplished something. He enjoyed the counseling sessions with the kids he worked with too, of course, but it was often harder to quantify what they got done there. On the ranch, things were a lot more straightforward. He knew that was part of why his plan for his farm had come to him. He'd thought football was his life growing up, but he'd come to the realization that part of his love for the game was the numbers. Success—or failure—was measured in yards and statistics. It was easy to see where you were doing well or where you were falling down.

Life wasn't like that. He never knew where he stood with his father. Some days, Marty would be happy and proud, others he'd be pissed off or ignoring Jackson. Same with all his relationships. He'd been involved with women, of course, but hell if he could figure them out. And even with the kids he worked with he wasn't always sure where they were at. Some days were good, some bad. And he got it. They were all human. They were all entitled to emotions that fluctuated and didn't always make sense. But football and the numbers of the game had grounded him. Now, the farm work did the same. If he needed to get two fences mended, feed a hundred head of cattle, and go into town for a specific list of supplies, then he knew when he had gotten it done and how well.

So he welcomed the work on Coach's ranch and loved feeling the combination of fatigue and pride at the end of the day.

Plus, he was now anticipating tipping back a beer or two with some of his buddies.

But his stomach was in a knot.

The beer would be fine. It was the buddies he wasn't sure of.

He'd kept in touch with Carter and Jase. Carter had done a great job of keeping everyone up on everyone else. Even when Jackson hadn't wanted anyone in his business, Carter had been a persistent fucker.

But Jackson hadn't seen some of these guys in years and he knew he'd let them down. They'd won the championship anyway, something he'd been conflicted about when it happened —he'd been thrilled for them while being a little pissed that they hadn't seemed to need him after all—but what had happened went deeper than the championship game. He'd let them down. He'd let his emotions and hormones rule him, he'd let his cockiness talk him into something he'd known was trouble. But he'd never had consequences to deal with. Not any that mattered anyway.

Until Jenny.

Well, until Annabelle.

He'd abandoned these guys and he wasn't sure how they felt about him now. He'd also been a dick for the rest of their senior year and the following year, running fast and hard, pushing every limit, not keeping in touch, not coming home.

Proving to the town he'd changed was necessary for his future employment here. But proving to these guys that he'd changed was necessary to his future *happiness* here.

He was glad Jase had insisted they all get together beyond the passing one another on the ranch or in Coach's house here and there as they all worked to keep things running.

And if he could keep his mind off of Annabelle, that would help.

God, he couldn't remember being so tied up over a woman before. She was on his mind constantly.

He'd been good. He hadn't gone to her house, he hadn't done anything more than meet her for coffee and text her.

But he'd wanted to.

So damn bad.

He wanted to be with her constantly—naked and not—and that was *not* according to plan. They were dating. He never saw the women he dated every single day, multiple times a day. Hell, the texting he was doing was already more than he usually did. Besides, it was supposed to be a quick, hot, didn't-mean-much fling that ended before school started. If they saw each other all the time and people started to see how she affected him, there would be no way they'd buy a breakup in only a couple of months.

He needed to be cool about this.

Or at least, *act* cool about this.

He saw Jase wave him over and started for the big round table in the corner. Several of the guys were already there. Even Nolan. Nolan Winters had moved to San Antonio and was now an award-winning journalist and a New York Times bestselling author, but he made it back to Bad on a fairly regular basis to see his mom and friends.

Jackson hadn't kept in touch with Nolan, but he had his first book. He got a huge kick out of knowing a bestselling author.

Jackson felt himself smiling for the first time since getting out of his truck. He was at the table, a hand on the back of a chair, when he saw Michael LeClaire was there.

Fucking LeClaire.

Dammit.

Annabelle wanted him to invite Michael to her dinner party. To make it more casual. Uh-huh.

Annabelle wanted to date Michael. That thought, and the idea of making nice at a dinner party where he was supposed to be impressing school board members, had been boiling in Jackson's blood all day. Annabelle's reasons for inviting Michael made sense. Jackson still didn't want it to happen.

He might not be staying for more than a beer after all.

He scraped out the chair next to Jase and gave the obligatory greetings around the table. Luke Hamilton was also there, as were two new guys. Nick Silver was the new doctor in town and Christopher Gilmore was a physical therapist who had just moved to Bad.

They all settled in for some good beer and even better bull-shitting.

Jackson had missed these guys.

They were about thirty minutes, and two pitchers of beer in when a soft, feminine laugh floated to Jackson over the other noise and something made him turn.

Annabelle was sitting at one of the high tables near the bar with Randi.

She'd noticed him. She was watching him when he turned. And dammit if she didn't blush when he caught her looking.

He wondered if he'd ever get tired of making that girl blush.

He should give her a cocky wink or something but he couldn't bring enough cocky out. He wanted her. The realization hit him in the gut. He'd known it, obviously, on a cerebral level but now, looking at her across the bar, it hit him deeper.

He wanted her and he didn't want Michael LeClaire to have her.

Which meant he was already fucking this up.

He'd gotten involved with one nice girl in his life. Jenny Schneider. The age difference, the fact that she'd been his student teacher had had nothing to do with it. He'd wanted her and had gone for it and it had cost them both.

He'd made a deal with Annabelle. He couldn't screw it all up by wanting her too much.

"You getting what you need?" Luke asked Nolan.

Jackson tuned back into the conversation with some effort.

Nolan nodded. "It's going pretty well. Just getting started."

"Started on what?" Jase asked, saving Jackson from having to.

"Nolan's writing a book about Coach," Luke explained. "He's interviewing people around town, gathering old photos and articles and stuff. He wants to talk to all of us."

"No shit," Jase said.

Nolan nodded. "It's true. Coach's story is compelling. He's done a lot for a lot of people through football in this little town."

Jackson couldn't agree more. But Jackson was watching Carter with a frown. Because Carter was watching Annabelle.

"Does AJ look different to you?" he asked Jackson underneath the other conversation going on at the table.

Jackson scowled. "What do you mean?"

"She looks especially hot tonight."

Maybe hard orgasms did that to a woman.

Jackson so wanted to say "yeah, I fucked that look onto her face" but he held back. For one, Annabelle deserved better than that. He might be responsible for the look on her face, but he would never make her sound easy. He knew he was supposed to be telling the other guys about how hot she was, that she wasn't the good girl they all believed her to be, but there were two problems with that. One, she *was* the good girl they all believed her to be. There was definitely more to her than that, but she was every bit the sweet, kindhearted, smart woman they assumed. Two, and maybe even more of a problem, he didn't want them to know about the girl underneath those skirts and blushes. He didn't want Michael taking her out. And he didn't want Carter taking her out. Hell, he didn't want *anyone else* taking her out.

Yep, he was already fucking this up.

"What about you?" Nolan turned to Jackson. "I understand

you've only been back a few days and you're already ruffling some feathers around here."

Jackson pulled his attention back to the table of men. He sighed and shrugged. "What else is new?"

"What's this football camp thing about?" Nolan asked.

"Football camp?" Jackson repeated. "What do you mean?"

"Coach has been talking all about it," Luke said. "The thing you do with the at-risk kids?"

Coach was talking about his farm? That made Jackson sit a little straighter. "It's awesome. But it's not football," he said. "And it's not a camp. It's a self-sustaining farm. I take at-risk kids and give them a safe place where they can learn about being part of a team, and make something with their own two hands. We use everything we grow, and grow or make most of the things we need. We also sell to the surrounding communities and take on repair and maintenance projects."

"There's no football at all?" Nolan asked.

Jackson grinned. "Well, I wouldn't say that. I might have a half field leveled off and painted in one of the pastures."

They all laughed and nodded as if no one was a bit surprised.

"I heard you're bringing it here," Michael said.

Jackson had to work not to scowl at the other man every time he looked at him. Why did Annabelle want Michael? He was…a great guy. Jackson sighed. "I'd like to bring the program here," he said. "Bad is unlike anything some of these kids have ever seen before. I'd like to show them how a real community works."

"If you need anything, let me know," Marc said. "I'd be happy to get involved. Maybe we could use some of the food you grow here in the restaurant. Do some farm-to-table stuff to highlight what you're doing."

Jackson's eyebrows rose. "Seriously?"

"Sure. You're one of my teammates, man."

Jackson couldn't name the exact emotion that he felt at that moment, but Marc had given him his first affirmation that his plan wasn't the craziest thing he'd thought up in a while. Well, the first besides Annabelle. She seemed to think the idea was a good one too.

And that easily, he was back to thinking about Annabelle.

He wanted to get her naked again.

He coughed and shifted on his chair, resolutely *not* looking in her direction. "That would be great. I appreciate that. The kids would love it. I was thinking of seeing if Coach would want to come over and help out some too. I could keep an eye on him so he didn't overdo, but I know he misses coaching and, honestly, a lot of this is like coaching. Seeing where the kids are going wrong, correcting them, giving them objectives and helping them dig deep to meet them."

Luke nodded. "I think inviting Coach is a great idea."

The conversation took off as the guys all reminisced about their favorite Coach stories. They polished off three more pitchers as they laughed, joked and teased as if ten years had never passed.

The knot in Jackson's gut was completely gone by the time he glanced over at Annabelle's table again.

The girls were getting ready to leave.

Jackson immediately shoved his chair back and stood. He pulled a wad of cash from his pocket and dropped several bills onto the table. "Hey guys, I gotta get going." He didn't give anyone a chance to protest or ask any questions.

Maybe it was the beer, maybe it was the feeling of satisfaction that things with the guys were good again, maybe it was that she was wearing another skirt and he couldn't concentrate on anything other than the way she'd let him put her up against his car six nights ago and he'd been a good guy since then. Whatever it was, he was getting another taste of her. Tonight. Right now. It was probably that his ability to be a good guy had a definite time limit.

———

"That's so good," Annabelle said with a sigh as she watched Jackson talking and laughing with the guys. "He needed to reconnect with those guys."

Randi glanced over at the group of men. "God, have you ever seen so much gorgeous in one place?"

Annabelle shook her head. She wasn't focused on anyone but Jackson but a woman would have to be dead not to feel the waves of testosterone coming from the table.

That should concern her. The table was full of big, good-looking guys. Guys from Bad. Guys she should be interested in. But the only one she was paying any attention to was Jackson.

Dammit. She was messing this up. She was supposed to be a quick summer fling for him. She was supposed to be letting loose, maybe trying a few new things—like sex on top of a '69 GTO for instance—and showing the guys around here she wasn't a stuck-up goody-goody.

Instead she was falling for Jackson Brady.

God, how stupid was that?

And how could it even be true? He'd been home for just over a week. They'd been getting along for about four days. And yet...

"Hey, how about margaritas and pedicures?" Annabelle asked. "I'll text the girls."

The girls referred to Regan and Priscilla. She could even talk Sabrina and Brooke and Daisy into girls nights in a while. "The gang" as her mother called them. Annabelle felt very lucky to have them. She'd preferred her books to real people; she'd spent Friday nights at home. Her parents had never given her a curfew because she'd never gone out. She was sure the thought had never even occurred to them. Her parents had been older when they'd had her. Her father was a college history professor in nearby New Orleans and her mother had been a housewife. Their house had been quiet and serious. They'd had a television but it was used for news programs and the occasional History

Channel program. They'd had a radio but it was used for the talk radio her mother listened to.

Since coming back to Bad, though, Annabelle had been introduced to something she loved very, very much—girls' night *in*. She still loved her books, she still loved her quiet time, and the noisy bar scene could make her twitchy, but she loved sitting around with the girls and drinking wine or margaritas and joking and telling stories and talking about guys. Or, in Annabelle's case, listening to the other girls talk about guys.

Now she had a guy to talk about and she would love to have the girls' input. She was crazy to be feeling anything but lust for Jackson, she knew that, but maybe the girls could tell her how to stop feeling it. She had no experience in any of this. And maybe that was the problem. Maybe this really was lust and nothing more.

She definitely needed some girl talk.

She pulled out her phone and sent a text to Priscilla.

Want to come over for margaritas? Randi's with me. I'm inviting the other girls too.

Cilla: *Pjs on. Bra off.*

Annabelle grinned. That was pretty much code in their group that one of them was in for the night.

Annabelle: *Come without it. It's just us girls.*

Cilla: *Rain check.*

Dang. She glanced at the table of men. Guess it was another night of just thinking about Jackson and trying not to.

Another text came in. *Jackson driving you crazy?*

Cilla knew her well.

Annabelle: *I'm so stupid.*

Cilla: *How so?*

Annabelle: *I really like him.*

She *liked* him. That didn't seem like a problem but she suspected it was. A fling was supposed to be physical. She was supposed to like his abs and his kisses and how fast he could separate her from her panties. Liking *him*, admiring him, finding him charming and funny…that was making things complicated.

It's the sex. Eyes on the prize, girlfriend.

The prize being what, exactly? A wild-child reputation? A new boyfriend? Michael? Suddenly none of that sounded so prize-like.

Annabelle: *I know. Hence the margaritas instead of more Jackson.*

Cilla: *I'll text you tomorrow.*

So no guy gossip tonight. Fine. Maybe she needed less focus on hot ex-football players who had panty-wetting smiles in general.

"Let's go. I need to stop at the store for strawberries." Annabelle slid off the stool and pulled her purse strap onto her shoulder.

"Uh, I don't think we're doing margaritas tonight," Randi said, focused on something behind Annabelle.

"Why no—"

Annabelle started to turn but the deep voice that said, "Annabelle" could only belong to one person. All of her girl parts recognized him immediately. And were very happy to hear from him.

She swallowed hard and turned to face Jackson.

"Uh, hi." Was that soft, husky voice hers?

"I'd like to take you home."

There was something in his expression that made her heart start beating harder. "Um, we were going to make margaritas."

"I've got something better."

Randi gave a low whistle behind Annabelle. So she saw whatever it was in Jackson's face too.

"Another kiss on the cheek?" Annabelle asked, then kicked herself. She couldn't let on that she was taking this too seriously. She wanted him to consume her body, mind and soul like the other night and then she wanted to wake up with him and make pancakes in the morning.

She was losing her mind.

Jackson, on the other hand, had signed on for a mutually beneficial fling and he'd been perfectly playing his part when he'd kissed her cheek.

And that was what was bugging her—he'd been playing a part.

How much of the rest of this was for show?

All of it.

That was how it was supposed to be. That was what they'd agreed on. Just because *she* kept forgetting it wasn't real, didn't mean he wasn't fully in character right now. But she was responding to him as if he was her long-lost love and that was a surefire way to get her heart smashed.

He leaned in. "I'll kiss you wherever you want me to."

Uh-huh. She crossed her arms, working on not reacting. It had been almost a week since he'd even put his hand on her butt. He was sweet and gentlemanly in public, but she was supposed to be getting the naughty side of him in private. Wasn't she? What about that part of the deal? And if this was all big talk for the sake of their audience, she was going to get cranky. Or cranki*er*.

If this was what it felt like to be sexually frustrated, maybe she was glad she hadn't been involved with someone like Jackson before. And how could she be sexually frustrated anyway? It had only been five days, twenty-two hours and sixteen minutes since she'd had sex.

She was definitely losing her mind.

She licked her lips and his gaze followed her tongue. "I thought maybe you'd gotten all of that out of your system the other night or something."

Were her feelings hurt? Was she feeling prickly because he'd been able to stay away? Was that what was going on? Pathetic. Seriously.

"Babe, a guy never gets *that* out of his system."

He gave her a wicked little grin and she tingled, as if she were a trained dog or something.

"Your self-restraint is admirable then." She sounded a little prissy that time. What was going on? Oh yeah, she liked him. And she wanted more than coffee and texts and kisses on the cheek.

"I do have a lot of self-restraint," he agreed. "But it's used up. Let's go."

"Why have you been trying to restrain if it was so good?" she had to ask. Pathetic though. And she fully expected Randi to smack her on the back of the head for it.

"I've been trying to be a nice guy." Jackson moved in closer and his voice dropped lower.

"Why the change of heart tonight?" Why was she poking him about this? Change of heart or not, this was good. Maybe it was an act but *this* was the part of the script that was about her. Having him look all possessive and hungry was a good thing.

Too bad she didn't care one bit what the other guys were thinking about all of this.

"Turns out I can only fake the nice guy thing for so long," he said.

"And you're done with it now?"

He leaned in, dragging a finger down the side of her face. "You have no idea how done I am."

Her entire body heated and she felt herself lean toward him too. Act or not, she could enjoy it, right? "I might have a few places I'd like to kiss too."

His gaze dropped to her lips, then came back to her eyes. There was a heat in his eyes that she was growing addicted to. "I might let you, too, if you ask really nice."

"Oh, right, the bossy thing."

His mouth quirked at the corner again. "Yes, the bossy thing."

"I don't know, the margaritas are tempting."

He reached for her hand and lifted it to his mouth, kissing the inside of her wrist. He flicked his tongue along the pulse point then murmured, "Please, Annabelle." He tugged her a little closer and kissed the skin a few inches above her wrist. "Please, Annabelle." His voice was lower and softer now. He pulled her closer again and kissed the inside of her elbow. "Please, Annabelle." He was almost whispering now.

And apparently there were parts of her that hadn't yet tingled. But they were now.

This was sweet and romantic and...strange.

"Are you drunk?" she asked

He traced a finger over the tattoo on her inner wrist, where he'd kissed earlier. "You got me so worked up the other night I didn't even get to look for all your ink."

She took a shaky breath. "You can look all you want right now."

His gaze bored into hers. "I'm not drunk. But I should warn you that I'm wound tight and I'm trying to restrain my caveman side, but I don't have a lot of practice with that."

She tipped her head. "Caveman side, huh?"

"Oh yeah."

To a liberated modern woman that would probably be a turn-off. Then why did the tingles increase? She cleared her throat. "What's that look like?"

"Me throwing you over my shoulder and carrying you out of here."

Her eyes widened and, if she wasn't mistaken, even her pinky toes tingled. Damn.

"Figuratively," she said.

"Oh no, very literally. And that would most definitely get some attention, wouldn't it? The guys in here would take note of that for sure."

She kind of wanted to see that. What did that say about her? "You wouldn't do that."

"I absolutely fucking would do that. And I think you'd like it."

She tried to look nonchalant. And very likely failed spectacularly. "Why do you think that?"

"Because you really liked my bossy side the other night and that was only the beginning of the caveman stuff I've got."

Yes, she really had. Dang. What did a girl have to do to get thrown over a guy's shoulder?

"Oh my God, I'm going to douse you both in ice water if you don't get out of here right now," Randi said. "And I'm totally jealous."

Jackson was still holding Annabelle's wrist. "You have good friends."

Annabelle couldn't agree more. She owed Randi a lot of chocolate. And booze. Maybe chocolate booze.

"I guess my plans have changed," she said flippantly.

"Damn right they have." Jackson still held her by the wrist so when he turned and headed for the door, he pulled her along with him.

She glanced back at Randi, who was grinning widely. Then she looked over at the table of Jackson's friends. Several of them were watching too. Including Michael.

She tripped a little over her feet and felt Jackson's arm go around her waist, holding her up and keeping her moving.

"Yeah, he sees it," Jackson muttered.

She looked up. The playful, sexy Jackson had been replaced by a determined, almost angry one. "Hey." She tugged on her hand but Jackson didn't even slow down.

He pushed the door open, towing her with him, and they stepped out in front of the Bad Brews.

"*Hey*," she said more firmly, digging her heels in this time.

"What?" He was frowning when he stopped and turned back.

"I'm leaving with *you*."

He scowled. "Damn right you are."

"And I'm not wishing for anyone else. I want to be with *you* tonight. I've wanted to be with you all week."

He stared down at her, his jaw tight. "I've been trying to be a good guy."

She nodded. "You keep saying that."

"It's true."

"But you're not doing a very good job at it."

He sighed and dropped her hand. "What a shock."

She laughed and moved in close, putting her hand on his chest. "What I mean is, a guy who was concerned with being *nice* to me would've given me another orgasm, or ten, long before this. I'm dying here."

The heat flared in his eyes and the mischievous grin was back. "Well, we can't have that, Ms. Hartington."

"That's better."

"I'll show you better." He dipped his knees, grabbed her butt, put his shoulder into her midsection and lifted her over his shoulder.

"Jackson!"

"You're all mine. All night. Hope you don't have anywhere to be early in the morning."

She'd cancel if she did. As if she could think right now.

The caveman thing really did do things to her.

CHAPTER
NINE

HE PUT her into the passenger seat of his car and jogged to the driver's side. They tore out of the parking lot a moment later and it was Annabelle's turn to grab the dash. They didn't talk as they drove to her house, pulled into the driveway and made their way up the front steps to the porch.

Annabelle fumbled with her key in the lock for a moment, her hands shaking. Her mind was filled with things like Jackson's hands and lips and other wonderful parts of him and the things she hoped he would do to her with those parts and—

"You're killing me here." He nudged her out of the way with his hip and took the key, inserting it smoothly and opening the door.

He pushed her inside, stepped in behind her, slammed the door and turned her back against it.

He lifted her wrist again and looked at the tattoo on the inner surface. "Letter b?" he asked.

"A flat."

"A flat?" He shook his head. "Don't know what that means."

She smiled. "A musical flat."

"Ah, music again." He looked down at her foot. "And that's a…"

"Treble clef sign."

"I'm sensing a pattern."

She nodded.

"So the treasure hunt begins." He put his hands under her shirt and swept it up and over her head.

Annabelle shivered. No wonder she was sexually frustrated. A simple touch, a few words, a heated look from Jackson and she was feeling all warm and melty all over.

He unhooked her bra and tossed it over his shoulder, his gaze roaming up and down her body. He wouldn't see any tattoos from this viewpoint but there was no missing the way her nipples beaded for him, begging for his touch.

He complied. He lifted his hands, cupping both breasts and rubbing his thumbs over the sensitive tips. Her head fell back against the door and she moaned.

"God, you're pretty," he murmured. He lowered his head and took one nipple in his mouth, licking then sucking firmly.

Her hand grasped the back of his head, her fingers sinking into his thick hair, holding him in place. "*Jackson.*" She felt the pulling desire deep in her pelvis and she wanted, *needed*, pressure there.

But he let her nipple go and lifted his head. "I've only found two. You said there were eight."

She could barely lift her eyelids. She nodded lazily. "Six more."

"It was dark the other night. I'm blaming that for missing a few." His hands went to her hips and he turned her.

Annabelle braced her hands on the door as Jackson brushed her hair over one shoulder.

"Ah-ha." His lips met her shoulder blade where a third tiny tattoo was printed. "What's this one?"

She felt the pad of his finger brush over the ink. "Musical notes." They were actually four eighth notes on the lines of a music stanza.

"I like this." His fingers running over the tattoo made goose bumps dance down her arm.

She breathed deeply. "Thanks."

"I'm going to want this story, but I've got more to find."

She felt his thumbs tuck into the waistband of her skirt on both sides.

"And I'm guessing, since I didn't get this all the way off of you the other night, that there might be some hiding under this skirt."

He pushed the skirt to the floor.

"And look at that."

She felt him kneel behind her. His big hands grasped her hips and brought her back against his lips as he kissed the quarter note in the dimple above her right buttock.

"Another note?"

She nodded.

He was quiet for a moment and she imagined he was scanning her body for more tattoos. He wouldn't find anymore back there—

He suddenly turned her so her back was against the door again. But this time, on his knees, he was eye level with her belly.

Jackson must have noticed a tiny bit of ink peeking out of the top of her panties, because he tugged them down, letting them drop to the floor. Annabelle stepped out of them and noticed that his gaze bounced between the two eighth notes on her left hip and the area between her legs where she *really* wanted his attention.

Big hands cupped her butt and brought her forward. She held her breath, thinking she would have his tongue on her clit any second, but instead he pressed his lips against the notes.

He did take a long, ragged breath, though, as if resisting more was difficult.

His gaze raked over her then, taking in every inch. She saw

his eyes widen when he saw the tiny note under the bone of her left ankle.

"How'd I miss that?" He lifted her foot to kiss the quarter note.

The position, of course, parted her legs and gave him an eyeful when he looked up.

Again, he did that long, deep breath and even licked his lips, but he didn't put his mouth where she needed him.

"There's one here too," she said, wanting to hurry him along now. She turned slightly to show him the small stanza that wrapped from the outside to the inside of her right thigh. It was longer than the others and was high enough to be hidden by skirts and even most pairs of shorts. Jackson leaned in and dragged his tongue along the ink, his mouth coming so, so close to her clit.

But he stopped short.

"One more," he said gruffly, looking up at her.

She raised her left arm to show him the tattoo on the underside. Another small stanza with a quarter note.

He stretched to his feet and wrapped his hand around her wrist, pressing it back against the door and pulling her arm over her head. The position showed off her tattoo and arched her breast closer to him. He dipped his head and kissed, then licked the tattoo. It was the feeling of being held in place and the dark look of desire when he lifted his head, though, that made heat flood through her.

He again lowered his head to her breast, sucking her nipple into his mouth.

"Damn you're sweet," he muttered as he shifted to her other breast. "I want every inch of you."

"*Yes*," she hissed.

He grasped her other wrist and pulled it up over her head too. "Clasp your fingers."

She threaded her fingers together.

"Leave your hands there," he told her, going to his knees. "If you move them, I stop."

He kissed the tattoo on her hip again.

"Understand?"

She nodded and licked her lips.

"Say 'yes Jackson'."

To hell with being liberated. She needed his mouth on her now. She'd do anything. And she suspected he knew it.

"Yes, Jackson."

"Very good." He ran his big, hot hands up and down the backs of her legs, cupping her ass and squeezing. His gaze was focused on her center.

She was hot and wet and willing to beg.

"Please, Jackson."

He lifted his gaze. "Please what?"

"Please do it."

He gave her a small smile. "I want to hear it, Annabelle. Tell me what you want."

"Kiss me."

He rose slowly, his body—his still completely clothed body—brushing against her bare skin all the way up.

He took her face in his hands. That wasn't what she meant but when his dark eyes met hers, she caught her breath. The hunger and possessiveness she saw there couldn't possibly be for show now. There was no audience. And she could *feel* it.

Jackson took her mouth slowly at first. He brushed his lips against hers, then pressed gently. He repeated the gentle kisses several times. And even those soft touches had her wiggling against him.

Annabelle knew that if she could get up against the roughness of his jeans, she could go off. She arched her hips closer to him, widening her stance slightly and seeking some pressure against her clit.

"You want it that way?" he asked, reading her actions perfectly. He grasped her thigh in one big hand and lifted it to his hip, pressing close, the hard bulge of his erection against her clit. "You want to get off like that?" he asked, moving her hips up and down. "Do it then," he said huskily. "Rub yourself to orgasm against me. Take what you need."

She wanted his mouth, his fingers, his cock, but she was almost mindless with desire. She needed relief. She arched against him again, feeling the denim grazing her sensitive flesh. She needed more. She started to move her hands, but Jackson's hand was there, trapping her wrists.

"Oh no," he chided. "Move those gorgeous hips against me, Hotshot. Work for it."

She whimpered, but couldn't stop herself. She rose on tiptoe, then let herself down, her clit rubbing against the coarse fabric and the rock-hard cock behind it. She repeated the action a few more times, feeling slight relief. But it wasn't enough.

"Fuck that's hot," Jackson breathed.

That spurred her on. She pressed even harder against him and his hips sank into her, pushing her more firmly against the door and putting delicious pressure against her clit.

"Jackson," she gasped.

"That's right," he coached. "You know what you need. Take it."

She widened her stance even farther and tugged hard against his hand holding hers to the door. "I need... I want..."

She couldn't even form words. Her orgasm was *right there*. She almost had it, but the pressure kept coiling tighter and tighter and wouldn't let go.

She lifted her head and sealed her mouth to Jackson's, needing *something*. His tongue swept into her mouth immediately, stroking bold and hard, in just the way she wanted between her legs. Her inner thighs tightened and she climbed a little closer to the summit.

Jackson let go of one of her wrists to cup the back of her head and tip her to deepen the kiss. That hand went to his shoulder and she used it to pull herself higher on his body. Instinctively, his hands went to her ass, holding her up. This spread her thighs and allowed all of her, clit and all, to be against his denim-covered cock.

She moved herself up and down on him, spread wide, the pressure perfect, and within moments, *finally* her climax broke over her.

She pulled her mouth from his and cried out his name, those amazing, delicious, addictive waves coursing through her.

"Fuck yeah," was Jackson's heartfelt response.

She opened her eyes to find Jackson staring at her, his jaw tight, the desire in his eyes enough to amp up the final few ripples of her orgasm.

"Need you, Annabelle."

"God, yes."

He reached between them to free his erection, the backs of his knuckles brushing against her hot, wet core.

She sucked in a quick breath. She wanted more, again, already.

He was fumbling between them, one hand still on her ass holding her up, the other trying to get a condom on.

"I'm on the Pill," she told him breathlessly.

His head snapped up.

She nodded. She'd been on it for years to regulate her crazy periods. She'd never been happier to have a wacky cycle than she was at that moment.

"Thank God." He moved his hand and thrust.

He filled her deep and hot, stretching her, hitting every single nerve ending that needed him so much.

She gasped and tightened around him, hanging on as he began to move.

"God, I love fucking you," he breathed hotly against her ear.

She loved the dirty talk. He said things that she'd never dream of saying out loud, or hearing for that matter, not to mention liking. Men didn't talk to her like this. But this was Jackson, he was this guy, a guy who got gritty and graphic and she'd had no idea how much that would fire her blood. But it wasn't the words alone, it was the hoarse need in his voice, the way his hands gripped her like he was barely holding back, the way he took over every one of her senses.

She also loved that he wasn't careful with her. He clearly didn't see her as the prim and proper English teacher everyone else saw—and who she admittedly had been before he came to town—and it made her want to let loose even more.

She wanted to consume him like he did her. She wanted to shock and please him, she wanted to be on his mind all the time, she wanted to be wanton and wild for him. He'd let all of this loose in her in just a few days. They'd only had sex twice and she was ready to give him anything.

That should scare her. But didn't. Not one bit.

She knew she could never tame him, she wouldn't want to, but she *really* wanted to keep up with him, to be what he wanted and needed, to fulfill his fantasies and keep him satisfied.

Damn, she was in deep.

Annabelle wrapped her arms around him and buried her face against his neck.

Jackson thrust into her, long, steady strokes that wound her tighter and tighter.

"That's right baby," he urged. "Take all of me."

She wanted all of him. *All* of him.

"Need you with me. Come for me, sweetness."

She felt the grip of her orgasm begin, pulling him in deeper and harder.

"Fuck yeah," he groaned.

And she came apart, again calling out his name, her whole body clamping down, never wanting to let him go.

His fingers curled into her, holding her still for his pounding thrusts, and moments later, he came fast and hard, growling her name.

The waves of pleasure took nearly two minutes to dissipate.

Jackson kept them propped against the door as he took in long breaths with hers.

Their bodies cooled slowly, their heartbeats coming back to normal gradually.

Finally he pushed away from the door and turned, striding with her across the room and dropping onto the couch with her on top of him.

She was fine with that. Unplastering herself from him was the last thing she wanted to do.

Ever.

Damn.

She again put her face against his neck, breathing in his scent, letting the heat from his skin soak into hers.

Jackson ran his hands up and down her back. "Tell me about the tats."

She loved the rumble of his chest against hers when he spoke. She turned her head, resting her cheek against his chest. She traced her finger over the tattoo that encircled his upper bicep. It was a swirling design that wrapped all the way around and made his already massive arm look even bigger.

"It's a song," she told him. "The first two stanzas, anyway."

"What song?"

"*Heart and Soul.*"

He didn't reply and she turned, folding her hands on top of his chest and propping her chin on them. "Have you seen the Tom Hanks movie *Big*?" she asked.

"A long time ago."

"It's the song they play on the big piano in the toy store." She hummed the first part.

He grinned at her. "You have a thing for Tom Hanks?"

She laughed. "I think he's a brilliant actor, but that's not why I have the song tattooed all over my body, no."

His hands kept stroking up and down her back and Annabelle felt herself growing warm and relaxed. She focused on his chin and the dark stubble that was starting to come in.

"Then why?"

"My mom and dad." She gave him a little smile. "My mom plays the piano beautifully. My dad doesn't have a musical bone in his body. But mom taught him to play that one song. It's a duet. Every time they had an argument or my mom got upset, she would go and play the piano and eventually my dad would join her on the piano bench and they'd play *Heart and Soul* and I would know that everything was going to be alright."

Jackson's hands settled on her butt. "I knew there was something special about your tattoos."

She looked up at him. "How?"

"You're not the spontaneous, get-drunk-and-inked kind of girl. You think things through, you do things with purpose, the things you do matter to you and mean something."

She thought about that. That all sounded very much like a conservative, well-respected, *nice girl*. But, for a change, that didn't bother her. Because he was right. She did do things with purpose, the projects she took on mattered to her and meant something, and she wasn't spontaneous. Even the fling with Jackson had taken her a day or so to decide.

And suddenly she thought she should point that out.

She lifted her head farther. "You're right. I don't do things that don't mean something and I do think them through." She met his gaze, wanting him to see the sincerity in her eyes. "Like this, with you. This isn't an accident."

Sure, she was overcome by the things he made her feel, but those things included liking him and wanting him to get the recognition and acceptance that he needed here and admiring how far he'd come and the things he'd done over the past few years. It wasn't just the sex. It was who he was. And if her well-thought-out, careful approach to life and the things and people she let into her life could help him see that, then she would be more than happy to be the conservative, uptight English teacher Bad wanted her to be. It wasn't only about convincing Bad that Jackson Brady was a good guy...it was about showing Jackson.

"You planned to have sex on the hood of my car and to get fucked up against your front door tonight?" he asked.

The graphic word shot heat through her as usual, but she ignored it. He was using it now to create distance. If he called it fucking, then that was all it was. She got it. But she wasn't going to let him do that.

"I knew what I was getting into when I suggested our deal," she said. "I knew it would lead to hot, amazing sex. And I wanted that. With *you*. I could have gone up to any other guy and told them what I wanted."

He frowned at that and Annabelle felt a little thrill in her chest. She liked him possessive.

"But you haven't. In all this time. You've been living here for eight years."

"Exactly. It was *you* who made me finally brave enough to say and go after what I wanted."

"It's chemistry," he told her, squeezing her ass. "We have a lot of it, I'll grant you. But you didn't really know me when you suggested all of this."

"I did. I'd read your file before you even set foot in my classroom," she told him. "And I definitely knew you when I wrapped my legs around you against my door tonight."

Heat and something else—hope, maybe?—flared in his eyes. When she put it that way it sounded a lot more like she'd opened herself up for him, chosen to let him get that close and be that intimate with her.

She didn't need a psych degree to see that he needed that. Jackson needed to know he was accepted, wanted exactly as he was right now without proving anything else.

He stared at her for a long moment and she met his gaze, unblinking. She'd never considered herself especially tough or stubborn. She'd never needed to be. Her family was easygoing, her friends were laid-back and her students were respectful.

But with Jackson, it was very likely she was going to need to be both.

"Teach me to play *Heart and Soul*," he finally said.

Her heart squeezed. He knew what the song represented for her—her parents' love and forgiveness toward one another.

Jackson was an insightful, caring guy. He might not show it all the time, but he had a sweet streak. He wanted to connect with people. He was close to Coach, reconciling with his old teammates had mattered to him, and he reached out to at-risk teens every day. He needed close relationships, he wanted that. He wouldn't suggest the song if he didn't want to be close to her.

Annabelle simply nodded and pushed herself up from where she was sprawled over his big, hot body. She padded across the floor and pulled her top and skirt back on without a bra and panties, and then held her hand out to him.

Jackson rose from the couch, he pulled his jeans up, but didn't bother to button or zip them. They rode tantalizingly low on his hips, the bulge behind the fly still impressive even when not fully aroused. Annabelle swallowed and focused on walking to her baby grand without tripping over her tongue.

She slid onto the bench, making room for him. He took up a lot of space on the bench and they ended up pressed tightly together.

She tried to focus, but was grateful that the song was simple, the same note pattern repeated over and over again. She played through the first two lines with the main melody.

"Here's your part." She put her right hand over the keys and showed him, slowly, what he was to play.

He tried to mimic what she'd shown him. He got the first three notes—which were the same note repeated three times —right.

She laughed and showed him again. She had to reach across him to get to the right keys. "Here, try it again."

He did. And messed it up.

She leaned in again, jabbing him in the stomach with her elbow as she angled to hit the keys.

"There's not enough room." He grabbed her and lifted her onto his lap.

Heaven help her, but she loved how he manhandled her. She settled onto his thighs, the bulge of his cock nudging her butt. His arms came around her.

"Show me again," he said gruffly.

She put his hand on the keys and covered it with her own. She pressed the keys down with her fingers on his.

"Okay, let me try." He got six of the eight first notes that time.

"Do it again." She played with him twice more, then let him do it on his own. This time he got it.

"Now play it again and again," she told him.

He played it twice through, fumbling only one note. Annabelle shifted to put her hands lower on the keyboard and began to slowly play the melody that went with Jackson's accompaniment. He stopped.

"Keep going. Hear your part, concentrate on the notes," she coached.

He started again and this time kept going as she played along.

It was slow and clunky, but they made it through once.

She grinned and looked over her shoulder. "There you go. *Heart and Soul*."

His hand moved from the keys to her stomach, his wide palm covering her, the heat seeping through the thin cotton of her shirt. "I like it."

She nodded. "Me too." She'd never shared her piano with anyone but the kids she taught. She didn't play for audiences, only for herself. Having him here, doing this with her, seemed strangely intimate. Especially that song.

He stared into her eyes. "Damn you smell good."

She pivoted on his lap to sit sideways, the bulge under her butt harder than it had been a minute ago. "You have to concentrate."

"No way. I can see your nipples poking against your shirt and when you lean over, I can see down your top."

She took a quick breath. "Jackson."

"And all I can think about is sucking on them again, making you moan and move against me." His fingers curled into her stomach. "I want you constantly. I want to be buried inside of you every minute of the day. I've never heard anything as good as when you say my name as you come."

Her whole body went hot and wet. That was what she wanted— for him to be crazy about her, to need her all the time like she did him.

"Jack—"

"I love this song, I love that you have the notes to it all over your body and I want to fuck you right here against this piano so that every time you sit down to play you'll think of me."

She couldn't breathe. Everything in her seemed to be straining toward him. She wanted that too.

But it was true. If she let him take her here, she would never sit at this piano—one of her havens, one of her special places— without thinking of him. Could she do that?

He cupped the back of her head and kissed her, long, deep, sweet.

She could definitely do it. She had to do it, in fact. If this fling, this whatever it was, was all she was going to have of him, then damn right she wanted to think about it every fricking day for the rest of her life.

She kept their mouths connected, but managed to turn fully, straddling his lap.

Jackson gathered her skirt up in his hands as she reached between them to free him from his jeans and boxers again. He was big and hard and ready for her and she thrilled with the thought that this man could want her so much.

He broke off the kiss, roughly pushing her shirt up, his hands going to her breasts, rolling and pinching her nipples, then plumping one breast as he lowered his head, taking it into his mouth with hard suction.

Annabelle wrapped a hand around his erection, squeezing and sliding up and down the length, wishing for the first time in her life that she could give a blow job.

But Jackson was giving her no time for that. He released her nipple and pressed her back so that she leaned against the keyboard behind her, elbows depressing the keys in a loud, dissonant chord.

He drank in the sight of her, running his hand up and down her torso, between her breasts. His breathing was fast and he had a wild look in his eyes. He lifted her skirt and brought her forward on his lap, but clearly he couldn't see what he wanted to.

"I'll buy you fifty more," was all he said before he grabbed the seam along the side of the skirt and yanked it apart. The skirt ripped up the side, the button closure at the waist popped open, and he flung it away.

Annabelle gasped and again realized that his rough dominant side was far more appealing that it probably should be.

"Caveman, huh?" she asked, her voice breathless.

"Damn right."

She was now wearing only her T-shirt, bunched up above her breasts.

"You're so fucking hot," he told her. Then he lifted her by the hips and brought her down on his cock.

The sudden thrust shot hot sensations through her body and she gasped. He was filling her completely and she still felt as if she needed more. She ground her hips against his, using the piano behind her for leverage.

"Yes, like that," he praised huskily.

He brought a thumb against her clit as he tugged on a nipple and Annabelle felt her orgasm already building.

She swiveled her hips and pressed against him again and he gave a little growl, squeezing her nipple. The sensation at her breast was seemingly linked to her clit and she felt the hot ache intensify.

"*Jackson.*"

"God, Annabelle."

His voice was needy and rough and even that made Annabelle's inner muscles clench in response.

"I'll never get enough of you."

Those six words sent her over the edge in the fastest orgasm she'd ever imagined. Her whole body clenched and she felt as though she was trying to pull him into her.

Including into her heart.

"Yes, fuck, yes," he chanted as he thrust up into her, the rhythm and power reflected in the loud, pounding notes from the piano.

He came, groaning her name, holding her tight against him as his body shuddered, and Annabelle leaned in, wrapping her arms around him.

And wondering how she was ever going to let him go.

CHAPTER
TEN

SHE MADE him pancakes in the morning and Jackson fell a little more in love with her.

Blueberry pancakes. After amazing sex in the shower, after hot-as-hell morning sex in an actual bed, after spending the night wrapped around her like she was a life preserver and he was in the middle of the ocean with no hope for rescue.

And damn if that wasn't a little how he felt.

He'd come home to Bad but he wasn't so sure he'd been *home* until he'd kissed Annabelle.

And what was he supposed to do about *that* when she wanted to go off and date her dream guy? Other than plow his fist into LeClaire's face, of course. Which was significantly less mature and enlightened than he'd been considering himself.

"Hear you're dating Annabelle Hartington."

Jackson froze three steps inside the doorway between Coach's kitchen and living room.

He'd just stored the casserole that his mother had sent along for Coach when Jackson had stopped by for a shower and change of clothes that morning. His mother might be sweet and able to delude herself into seeing only what she wanted to see about Jackson, but she was a hell of a cook.

That thought allowed his forced smile to seem a little more genuine. He nodded. "Glad to see the grapevine still works fast around here."

Everyone was supposed to know that he and Annabelle were dating. That was the point. But he'd always felt jittery when Coach knew something that Jackson was uncomfortable with.

He wasn't uncomfortable about Annabelle, actually. In fact, it almost seemed too comfortable. Too right. Too natural.

And *that* made him uneasy. He wasn't interested in getting his heart broken.

Coach didn't smile. Jackson straightened as he met Coach's gaze. "Someone told you because they're concerned," Jackson said. That shouldn't surprise him. He'd expected it on some level so it shouldn't hurt. But it still stung.

Damn.

"Yes. My daughter."

Jackson was surprised. Wild child Elyse was concerned? "Is that right?"

Of course, Elyse didn't really know him and she was feeling protective of sweet Annabelle. He could understand that.

"Elyse likes Annabelle."

Jackson nodded. That was exactly the point. But... "I like Annabelle too."

And it was the God's honest truth. Yes, he'd very much liked everything that had happened in—and on— his car and in and against her front door and piano and bed and shower. But it wasn't just the sex. The talking, the teasing, the way she lit up driving his car, the way her hair always seemed to be in her face, making her fuss with it constantly, the combination of innocent and naughty, the way she'd opened her body to him so easily, the fact that she was probably the smartest woman he knew and she was still spending time with him.

So many things. Dangerous things. Sex he could handle. Even sex that made his head spin and his stomach feel like he was on a roller coaster. The other things—the softer things, the way she made him smile, the way he wanted to impress her, the feel of her hair, the skirts, the tattoos that truly meant something to her—those things had tipped him off balance and he wasn't sure what to do.

Except send her flowers. Which he'd done on his way to his mom's place. And text her naughty but sweet notes during the day. And wait for her in front of the coffee shop every day.

It was all about the ruse. They were supposed to be dating. Those were dating things.

Even if the flowers had gone to her house, where no one else would see them, and even if the texts would only get seen by someone else if she showed them.

"Is it a coincidence that you're dating her immediately when you get back to Bad and want to impress everyone?" Coach asked.

Coach knew Jackson. Too well sometimes. Jackson might want to insist that things with him and Annabelle were all for show, but he couldn't with Coach. Coach could see through Jackson's bullshit faster than Jackson could make a bad decision.

And that was fast.

"I want people to know I'm different."

"Why?"

"Why? Because I want to live and work here. I want to start up another farm. I want to show them that I've changed."

"Are you sure you have?"

Jackson scowled at the man he trusted more than anyone on the planet. He and Coach had talked every single day since Jackson had been back in Bad, but they hadn't had one of their heart-to-hearts yet. Of course, Jackson had known it was only a matter of time. Those had been a weekly thing when Jackson was in high school and there was no way he wasn't going to do something stupid enough to deserve one even now. "Yes, I'm sure."

Coach accepted that with a single nod. "Then why do you care what they think?"

Jackson started to reply, his easily riled defensive streak riled up good, but he paused. "I..."

"Because you're *not* sure you've changed. You want them to think it so *you* can believe it."

Jackson stared at the older man. He wanted to argue. He wanted to deny it. But dammit... "Maybe."

"And it's because you haven't really changed that much."

Jackson went right back to scowling. "Thanks a lot."

Coach chuckled, the sound a welcome relief. Coach had chewed Jackson's butt many times. He'd held the mirror up to Jackson and made him really look at himself. He'd given him advice. But the best thing Coach had ever done was accept him. Not because he ran the football better than anyone in the state or because he knew exactly when to turn on the charm or because he was a hell of a good time. Coach saw the flaws, he saw the mistakes, and he accepted Jackson—loved him even—anyway.

His dad had looked at Jackson and seen an NFL paycheck since he'd been old enough to hold a football. What his dad saw now was just as simple— he looked no further than Jackson's fuck ups and his wasted potential. His mom had always looked at him and seen a good-looking kid who brought her flowers for no reason and told her she was beautiful and a great cook. It had always been so superficial with both of them. And not just with his own parents. He could impress almost any man with his football talents and hunting talk and charm almost any woman with compliments and a smile.

But with Coach it was real. He saw Jackson's shortcomings, the times he tried and failed, the things he *couldn't* do—backing down from a challenge for one, keeping his mouth shut for another—and Coach still cared.

Like Annabelle.

That thought hit Jackson directly between the eyes. Did he like her? Damn right he did. She was real. She saw his flaws. She knew he wasn't perfect. She wasn't impressed by football or hunting stories and she wasn't easily won over with charming smiles.

"Don't suppose it ever occurred to you that you didn't change that much because you were already pretty great?" Coach asked, reaching for his bottle of water. He winced as the motion pulled on his sore chest.

Jackson gripped his hands into fists, resisting doing it for him. Everyone agreed, including Coach, that he needed to do as much on his own as he could, that babying him along wasn't going to help. Still, it was hard watching him hurt.

"I don't know that I was already pretty great. I had a lot of growing up to do."

"You were a kid. A hot-headed, too-smart-for-your-own-good, manipulative, hormone-driven kid. But you were a good person underneath all of that."

Jackson snorted. "Well, it was *really* deep. There was a lot of crap to get through."

"But you did it," Coach said, firmly. "You got control, you figured out what you wanted, what was important. You let go of football as the be-all, end-all of your existence."

"Football let go of me." He would have never let it go. It had been everything. Was it good that he'd had to find other things to do to fulfill him? Sure. But losing the thing that had mattered the most had been like tearing out his heart.

"Bullshit," Coach said shortly.

"What?"

"You let it go. And you know it. You were always pushing to see what your dad would do, if he'd give a shit. The only thing that mattered to *him* was football. So you could get into all kind of trouble and never have any consequences. Until it affected football. You finally got what you wanted."

Jackson felt as though a tight iron band had wrapped around his chest. Coach was right. He'd finally figured that out for himself. The only thing about him that had ever mattered to his dad was his ability to play ball. He'd started peewee football when he'd been in first grade. That was when his dad started paying attention to him. The iron band squeezed and for a second he couldn't breathe. It was still the case. Since he'd been tossed off the team, he and his dad had spoken maybe a dozen words. Six of them had been at dinner his second night in Bad when he's said, "Hi, Dad, how are you?" and his dad had replied with, "Fine."

Coach watched Jackson's face and slowly nodded. "You want to talk about being a psychologist? Try coaching a bunch of teenage boys for thirty years or so."

The tight band around his chest let go with those words. Jackson's dad was a jerk. He always had been. It hadn't been Jackson's fault he couldn't measure up or be important to his dad. That was all on his father. He knew that.

But it made a difference that he mattered to *someone*. To Coach. To Annabelle.

"So what's Elyse concerned about exactly?" Jackson asked. Hell, he hadn't even known Elyse and Annabelle were friends. Elyse had been a couple of years younger than all of them. Of course, Bad was a small town. And Annabelle was Annabelle.

"Everyone likes Annabelle. She's a sweet girl. A great teacher. Someone a lot of people look up to."

Jackson shifted uncomfortably. Those had been some of the reasons his plan to date her had seemed so great. Just because it now felt like he had a dozen or so other very good reasons, didn't mean those things weren't still true.

"Annabelle and I are having a good time."

Coach nodded. "That's why Elyse is concerned."

"Because we're having fun?"

"Annabelle doesn't really have fun."

Jackson tried to gauge if Coach was using "fun" to mean more...like the bedroom kind of fun. "Well, now she is." Even if Coach *did* mean bedroom fun, Annabelle was having that now for sure. But Jackson would like to think she was having some additional fun, too.

"Annabelle's the marrying type." Coach pushed himself up from his recliner. It was a tough move for him and Jackson stood gritting his teeth, fighting the urge to haul Coach up himself.

Finally on his feet, Coach looked up at Jackson. "Elyse's afraid Annabelle's going to fall in love with you and that you're using her for a good time and to look good to the town."

Well, hell, it looked as if Coach wasn't the only one in his family who was insightful. But still, something inside of Jackson protested. It was crazy, stupid even, but he didn't feel like there was anything "only" about what he and Annabelle were doing.

"She's too smart to fall for me." His heart clenched a little as he said it though. Damn, having a woman like Annabelle let him do the things he'd done to her—and that he still intended to do —was a thrill. It was something he *needed*. To know that someone could trust him and need him for something. But to think that she might fall in love with him? That was amazing. Was he capable of being someone Annabelle could love?

And did he want that?

Coach pointed a finger at his nose. "Annabelle is smart. You got that right. So if she falls for you, and tells you she loves you, don't go thinking it's because she's inexperienced or easily won over or delusional. You believe her, got it?"

Jackson felt adrenaline shoot through his body. Coach seemed to think this was a real possibility. Annabelle was also the type of woman that a smart guy would love back. Did he want to be in love?

"And if you're smart, you'll take whatever she'll give you and hold on to it. She's not like your mom and dad, Jackson. She's not like your groupies. She's not like the boys you counsel. They only see part of you. She'll see it all." Coach narrowed his eyes. "Like me."

Jackson knew that was true. Coach saw it all.

"I'll be good," he promised.

"See that you are." Coach turned toward the kitchen. No doubt to grab a few Oreos to go with the fruit salad Elyse had left with strict instructions that it better be all gone when she stopped by later. "And for the love of God, quit looking like someone's yanking your nose hairs out every time I get up or move."

Jackson smoothed his expression even though Coach's back was to him—he'd always assumed Coach had eyes in the back of his head. Watching the man shuffle across the floor was killing him. Coach was supposed to stride, or stomp, or even run.

"I'm not dying. I've got a lot of years of kicking your butt still to do," Coach said as he disappeared around the corner.

Jackson let the tension ease from his shoulders and even felt a smile curl his lips. He might have grown up, he might even be capable of a real grown-up relationship, but there was no doubt that he still needed butt kickings from time to time.

The measure of how seriously he was taking the dinner party at Annabelle's was in the fact that he was wearing a tie.

He hated ties. He owned two and he hated the one he was wearing only slightly less than the one he'd left in his closet in Omaha.

He only had a tie along on the trip because he'd hoped to need it for an interview with the school board. Looked like he was going to need to make a good impression twice.

No pressure there.

But all thoughts of interviews and ties and school boards fled when Annabelle answered the door.

She was wearing a navy blue dress that was form fitted, hit her at mid-thigh and hugged her body. She wore her hair down and loose and had her eyes rimmed with dark liner. Her lashes looked longer and she wore lipstick as well.

He almost swallowed his tongue.

She stood in the doorway watching him take in the full picture.

When he got to the three-inch heels, all of his blood left his head for his cock.

"Holy shit, Annabelle." He somehow dragged his gaze back up to her face. "You trying to kill me tonight?"

She gave him a sly smile. "Maybe a little."

He'd created a monster.

He stepped in close, fully intending to kiss the hell out of her, but he heard a car door slam behind him. More guests had arrived. Probably for the best, considering if he got his hands on her now, they wouldn't be coming off her until she was naked and writhing against the wall in her foyer.

"Tonight, when I can't rip it off you and take you on the counter, is the night you decide to wear a dress that shows off your breasts and ass?" he asked low enough only she would hear.

She smoothed her hands down the dress. "You like it?"

She fucking knew he did. "Makes me want to bend you over the kitchen table."

She didn't even blink at that. Yep, he'd made her a siren.

"You wouldn't want to bend me over the table if I was wearing one of my usual skirts?"

"Well...I... Yeah, I would."

She grinned and stepped back so he could enter the house. Which he did, brushing way closer to her than he actually needed to. That finally got a little hitched breath from her. Damn right. She might be more confident and sexy than ever before but he could still affect her.

"Hope you're not planning to clean up right after dinner." He kept his voice quiet, covertly running his hand over her hip, aware of the people coming up the front path. "The minute that door closes behind the last guest, you're naked and spread out on that table."

"Not bent over?" She looked up at him through her lashes, the perfect picture of a siren who had the poor sailor in her clutches and knew it.

"Not the first time," he growled.

She laughed and Jackson felt something in his chest turn over. The teasing, the laughter—he loved it as much as making her scream.

Her attention focused on something over his shoulder and Jackson moved out of the way. "Welcome," she greeted Sally MacDonald and her husband Troy. "I'm so glad you could come tonight."

"This is so nice," Sally said. "Thank you for having us."

Sally was a lifelong resident of Bad and had been on the school board for a full term already. She was starting her second term in the fall, this time as president. But she was a woman and Troy was a football fan who liked to hunt. They should be easy for Jackson.

He also knew that Scott Conrad, another school board member, and his girlfriend Emma would be here tonight.

Scott had been about ten years ahead of Jackson in school and Emma was from out of town. Scott hadn't played ball and didn't hunt. He was a big-shot lawyer and basically considered himself above the beer and bullshitting that Jackson and his friends enjoyed. Scott might be tougher to win over.

For a moment his stomach clenched. He wanted to be himself. He didn't want to talk football. He didn't want to try to impress anyone. He wanted to talk about Bad high school, the kids, and his farm program.

Jackson smiled and greeted Sally and Troy and accompanied them into the living room. Annabelle had appetizers laid out on the coffee table and a selection of drinks on the small table near the fireplace. The house smelled amazing with whatever she'd made for dinner and Jackson was touched by the amount of work she'd gone to for him. He didn't do dinner parties. He did pizza nights and barbecues with the kids at the farm. He did wings and beer with his buddies once in a while. He ordered Chinese food for delivery about once a week. But no hors d' oeuvres, no chilled beer mugs and no ties.

Annabelle, on the other hand, seemed completely comfortable with this setting. No doubt she attended faculty parties and such. But she also had a natural grace and warmth that put people at ease. She was articulate and bright so could talk about any topic and she'd always been an observer, so she knew things, like the fact that Troy and Sally had a four-year-old grandson named Hunter, and that Scott Conrad and his girlfriend Emma, who had arrived just after Sally and Troy, had recently been on a cruise. She greeted Jase with a big smile and Priscilla with a hug. Michael also got a smile and Daisy another hug. Jackson appreciated that she had invited some friends to make things more comfortable and less like an interview. Though he would have had to be blind to miss how LeClaire checked her out.

Still, Jackson did not stalk across the room, jerk Michael around by the collar and slug him.

He was on his best behavior in general. He hadn't made up a reason he needed to see her in the other room so he could press her up against the wall for a moment. He hadn't given in to the nearly constant urge to loosen his tie. He hadn't let any fucks sneak into his conversations. At least not the ones he was having out loud with other people.

But his eyes were never far from Annabelle. He was perfectly content just to watch her. And imagine all the ways he was going to take her later when everyone left.

She was glowing. It wasn't as if he'd seen her at dinner parties before, but there was something about her tonight that seemed brighter, happier...a definite glow...that couldn't come only from entertaining.

Then Michael said something that made her laugh and Jackson's stomach clenched.

Fuck, he loved that sound. He'd never get tired of hearing it. But he wanted to be the one making it happen.

"Hi, Jackson."

Scott pulled Jackson's attention away from Michael and Annabelle.

"Hey, Scott." Jackson forced a smile. "Thanks for coming."

"Of course. I couldn't say no to one of our finest teachers," Scott said. "Annabelle doesn't ask for personal favors."

Jackson's eyebrows went up. "She asked you to come as a personal favor?"

Scott nodded. "Said she wanted us to learn more about the farm project she wants you to bring to Bad. She sent us a bunch of information and wanted to talk about it more tonight."

Jackson felt a tightness in his chest. Annabelle was telling everyone *she* wanted him to bring the program to town? She was putting her name in with the farm as well as with him personally. "I appreciate your interest."

Scott shrugged. "I'm intrigued anyway. I won't tell you I don't have some reservations. Probably would have flat-out said I wasn't in favor if it wasn't for Annabelle's interest."

Jackson worked on not frowning. "Reservations?"

"Well, you're planning to bring kids to Bad who are from very…different backgrounds."

Jackson did not hide his frown completely this time. "Different how?"

Scott laughed. "Growing up in the city is pretty different than growing up in Bad."

Jackson nodded. "Making Bad a great experience for these kids."

Scott shrugged. "Maybe. I guess I want to hear more about your plans for the kids. It sounded like your program in Omaha was more like an extracurricular program or after-school job."

"That's right. Though some of the kids stayed if they needed to."

"Annabelle was talking about possibly running it like a summer camp or even possibly a boarding program. Having the kids live at the farm and attend school here during the week and going home on the weekends," Scott said. "You can imagine that would bring up a lot of questions."

Several things occurred to Jackson at once. One, that a program like that would operate differently than the one he ran in Omaha and would take a lot more paperwork, permissions, licenses and so on. Two, Annabelle had given this a lot of study and thought and was talking about him and the program extensively.

That was...amazing.

He had support from city leaders and the school district administration in Omaha. He had law enforcement on his side and the parents' backing. He had friends who supported him, even giving financially.

But no one had ever pushed the program or been a strong vocal advocate for it.

Every time he thought he'd figured her out, Annabelle surprised him with something new.

He heard her laugh again and looked over.

Surprises like that damn dress.

Michael seemed to like it too. He hadn't moved from her side since he'd come through the front door.

Jackson frowned and again fought the urge to go over and insert himself firmly between them.

LeClaire was interested. Of course he was. Annabelle was gorgeous and sexy and now had that glowing thing going on that, very likely, came from having really good sex.

Jackson had induced that happy, sexy glow and it was now attracting other men.

As planned.

Fuck.

"Dinner is ready," Annabelle finally announced.

Everyone took their seats and Jackson made sure to put himself next to Michael on the other end of the table from Annabelle. Damn, he did *not* want to have this conversation. But he'd made a deal. Annabelle had held up her end. In fact, she'd gone above and beyond. She was most definitely making him look good to the people important for his future in Bad.

So he had to encourage Michael to ask her out.

And he would.

Later. Maybe after dessert.

Or next year.

"Damn, AJ looks amazing."

Jackson sighed and looked over at Michael. Or maybe they'd talk about it now. "She does."

"Too bad she's been hiding all of that."

Jackson looked back at Annabelle. He knew Michael was referring to her body, but the words hit him differently. She'd been hiding a lot and it wasn't just the delicious curves. She'd hidden her wit, her charm, her love for classic cars, her musical abilities, her soft heart.

And he knew that if she hadn't been hiding, he wouldn't have been the lucky one to uncover it all.

"You thinking about asking her out?" Jackson asked, the words tasting like acid in his mouth.

But he owed her this. She'd wanted a new image as much as he had.

"Me?" Michael chuckled. "I don't think so."

Jackson frowned. He didn't want Michael to ask her out, but he wanted Michael to *want* to ask her out. She deserved that. And Jackson wanted to know that one of the men he counted as a friend wasn't a complete idiot. "Why not?"

"I don't think I'm Annabelle's type."

"That, or you don't think she's *your* type?" Jackson had to ask.

"Maybe both."

"You might be surprised." Jackson hadn't meant to mutter that as if the entire idea royally pissed him off. But it did and he'd never been real great at hiding his negative emotions.

"Yeah?"

Jackson knew Michael's eyes were back on Annabelle. That's

exactly where his were as a humbling, and pretty fucking horrible, thought hit him—she hadn't dressed up like that for him.

The lipstick, the mascara, the hair, the push-up bra—that was all about Michael being here tonight.

And the glowy whatever-it-was in her face could be as much about anticipating seeing and showing off for LeClaire as it was because of anything Jackson had done to or with her.

Speaking of creating a monster...

"Why do you think you're here tonight?" Jackson asked Michael, his throat tight.

"I think I'm here because she wanted to bring a bunch of people together who could help you get this farm going. She's pretty excited about it. Hard to say no to that enthusiasm." Michael grinned. "And that was even before the blue dress. Now I'm not sure I'll ever say no to her about anything."

Jackson felt his gut tighten right along with his throat.

He shifted and told himself to settle down. This was the deal. She'd gone to a lot of work for him. She was putting herself and her reputation on the line when she asked for favors from these people and enthusiastically endorsed his farm. He'd agreed to help Michael see her differently. It was his own fault he had fallen for her. And as painful as it was to think about her in another's man's arms, there was only one thing worse...the idea of breaking a promise to her.

"You're going to be able to help me with the farm?" he asked Michael.

Michael turned toward him, resting an elbow on the table, his expression suddenly serious. "Annabelle's filled me in. Your program is impressive. And if Bad doesn't want it, Autre will welcome it."

Jackson looked at him in surprised. "Really?"

Michael nodded. "I understand there's some hesitation around here. Some...concerns." He cast a glance at Scott. "But I know Autre. That town is full of people who would embrace this program, Jackson."

"And you're on board?" Jackson asked.

Michael met his eyes, his expression sincere now, all joking aside. "Yeah, man. I'm on board. Whatever you need."

Jackson needed Michael to leave Annabelle the hell alone.

But if he couldn't have that, then he'd settle for Michael treating her well and making sure she knew how amazing—kind, giving, smart, sassy, gorgeous, sexy, sweet—she was every day that he had with her.

He watched her chatting with Daisy at the end of the table. He loved everything from her smile to the way she sipped her wine.

And he was going to encourage another man to date her.

Son of a bitch. He had maybe finally fully turned into a good guy.

As he'd always suspected—being a good guy kind of sucked.

His thoughts were broken up by Scott looking down the table at him.

"So, Jackson, you've been working for a school in Omaha, is that right?"

And the not-really-an-interview-interview began.

Jackson settled into his chair. He picked up his coffee cup and sipped, trying to act relaxed. He nodded. "I worked for the entire district counseling the more at-risk teens, those who have had run-ins with the law, ones where truancy is an issue, that kind of thing."

"Not guidance counseling then?" Sally asked with a slight frown.

Jackson worked on not looking uncomfortable with all the attention on him. This was what they were here for. "Not specifically, no. The schools each have a guidance counselor. I came in for more...complicated cases."

Sally looked at Scott then Jackson. "We don't have complicated cases here in Bad."

Jackson chuckled softly. Kids in small towns where everyone was in everyone else's business were just better at hiding their issues sometimes. "There are kids who need help everywhere. There's a spectrum, of course, and there are a number of programs that can benefit kids anywhere along that spectrum. I can be a resource for the staff and parents too."

Sally blinked at him. "But you want to be our guidance counselor?"

Jackson nodded again. "Yes. I'm qualified for that position as well."

"More than qualified," Annabelle added.

He gave her a smile. Having her on his side felt good.

"But you don't have experience," Sally said.

"I have six years of counseling experience in middle and high school."

Patience. That was one of those things he'd learned since leaving Bad.

Annabelle gave Sally a look. "If Jackson's been able to work with kids who are at risk for gang behavior or dropping out of school because of family issues, I'm sure he can handle helping kids apply for college."

Jackson tried to catch her eye. Her defense of him was sweet, but there was no need to irritate Sally.

"The kids here in Bad are very different from the ones Jackson's been working with," Scott said.

"That's true in some ways," Jackson acknowledged. "Most of the kids here have a much more stable base, not to mention the community behind them. But kids are kids on some level."

Sally didn't look convinced.

Great.

"So you think the would-be criminals you're planning to bring here are like the kids in Bad?" Sally asked.

Jackson felt his eyebrows rise and consciously put them back in a relaxed, unassuming position.

"Would-be criminals?" Annabelle repeated, her tone sharp.

Jackson caught her eye this time and shook his head slightly.

"I think there's some misunderstanding about my program," he said to Sally calmly.

Sally picked up her coffee cup. "Perhaps. But the whole town has the same misunderstanding. And if you think the kids in Bad are the same as those kids you've had on your farm, then I think perhaps *you* are the one with the misunderstanding."

"Jackson is helping give these kids a second chance," Annabelle said. "Everyone is jumping to conclusions without even knowing any details."

He couldn't help but feel warm at Annabelle's words. Any thought that she might have been saying good things around town for show only was quickly wiped clean at the look on her face. She was in full support of his program.

Jackson tried to smooth things over. "Sally, I would be happy to explain the program, get some letters of recommendation, maybe bring some of the kids here—"

"Or you could forget about the program, of course," Scott inserted.

"Asshole," Michael said under his breath.

Jackson glanced at the man beside him.

Fortunately, it seemed Jackson was the only one who'd heard him.

"I think it's safe to say that everyone would be happy to welcome you on board at the school if the program wasn't a factor," Scott went on.

"Not everyone," Michael muttered, looking at Jackson. "Just *one* asshole."

And with Michael's words something clicked inside Jackson.

Scott and Sally were only two people. Two people out of a whole town of people. Okay, Tom Thorpe hadn't been thrilled about the program either. So, three people.

Bad was a wonderful place. Full of great people. Some of those people were conservative and resistant to change. Some were even elitist and old-fashioned and judgmental. Some were just protective. But many—most even—were kind and generous.

Jackson probably should have been expecting this from Sally and Scott though. A program like his was something unusual for Bad and not everyone did well with unusual. His program was one of many in Omaha. This was new to Bad.

"Bad is a wonderful place." Jackson said it with sincerity he was sure Sally and Scott could see. "I went way off track but the people I knew and the things I learned in Bad brought me back. I think Bad could be a great influence on these kids who haven't had a true family unit, not to mention a community supporting them."

Sally gave him a small smile. "That's nice, Jackson." A small, insincere smile.

"I think you should let it go for now," Scott advised, finishing off his wine. "Get settled. Show people that you're interested in fitting in. Maybe down the road it will be different."

Right. Fitting in. That was the key, he knew. That was the part he was still working on.

If he could work with the kids in Bad and have a positive effect there, he'd have a better chance at gaining the town's trust for bigger projects.

"I appreciate the input, Scott," Jackson said.

Annabelle interrupted again. "I think peoples' impression of these kids are based more on assumptions than fact."

"Damn, she's even hotter all riled up," Michael said quietly.

He had no idea.

Annabelle hadn't even met the kids. She didn't know any more about the program than the people sitting around the table with them, and still she was defending him.

Being a good guy definitely sucked.

Scott took a swallow of coffee then looked at Jackson seriously. "Let's be honest."

Oh good, more honesty.

Jackson leaned forward in his chair but kept his expression calm. He hoped. "Great."

"You have some history to live down. You can understand

why some members of the community might be hesitant to let you loose with something new. Especially something that involves our young people. People who can be easily influenced by peer pressure."

"So you're concerned that the kids I would bring in from the city would negatively influence the kids here in Bad?" Jackson clarified.

"Yes," Scott said with a shrug.

"It is possible," Jackson agreed. Of course it was *possible*. "But peer pressure happens at all socioeconomic levels, in every school, in every country. I'd argue that giving the kids a new perspective, a chance to meet people from different back-grounds, would add more positives than negatives."

"Not sure it's worth the risk," Scott said simply.

Sure, fuck research, fuck experience, fuck common fucking sense… Jackson made himself breathe and not react.

"Michael," Annabelle said sharply.

Michael looked up, a forkful of pasta suspended between his plate and mouth. His gaze flickered around the table. "Uh, yeah?"

"What do you think of Jackson's project? You're not from here. You're more objective," Annabelle said.

Crap. Jackson sighed. What was she doing?

Michael had been keeping his voice down on purpose. Jackson appreciated the other man's words, but he understood that Michael didn't want to go head to head with Scott in Annabelle's dining room.

But Michael put his fork down, wiped his mouth with his napkin and nodded. He looked at Jackson, then he looked at Annabelle. "I trust Jackson," he said. "And you. I know you wouldn't be behind it if there was anything to worry about."

Well, there it was. Michael was a good guy.

And he liked and respected Annabelle.

And he had finally noticed Annabelle was hot.

That's what Jackson needed to know.

"Annabelle, isn't it time for dessert?" Jackson asked.

She looked startled for a moment. She glanced around the table and Jackson knew she was going to say no. Until she met his eyes. She read exactly what he wanted her to. He wanted to talk to her in private.

She scooted her chair back. "Yes it is. I tried a new cheesecake recipe," she told everyone with a smile.

"She can make cheesecake too?" Michael said to Jackson.

Jackson's jaw tightened, then he did the hardest thing he'd ever done in his life. He looked at Michael and said, "Come find us if we're not out in ten minutes."

CHAPTER
ELEVEN

AS SOON AS the kitchen door bumped shut behind her, Annabelle whirled to face Jackson, arms crossed, blocking any escape. Unless of course he picked her up and moved her out of the way.

Jackson leaned against the counter across from her, gripping the edge.

"You're caving?" she asked, completely exasperated.

"I'm not caving. I'm being patient."

Scared was not the same thing as patient. Annabelle hated this. Cautious, conservative, patient—those weren't who Jackson was. His passion was sometimes a little out of control, but it was real. Because of that, it could be trusted. For a woman whose life had been very quiet and controlled, Jackson was like a breath of fresh air. When someone got worked up, you knew what they felt, what they cared about. When they were controlled and careful, they could hide.

"They're preying on the fact that you feel like you let everyone down here and you don't want to do it again," she said bluntly. And frankly, she understood where Scott and Sally were coming from. When she looked at it objectively, some of their concerns made sense. But this was Jackson. He wasn't supposed to care what they thought and then he was supposed to amaze them by proving them wrong. "You can't feel that way. What you want to do with the program is amazing and this town will just have to get over it and—"

"Annabelle."

But she wasn't stopping. She never ranted and raved and it felt good. Her heart was thumping, her blood was hot and she had an overabundance of energy to let loose.

"Your *passion*, your willingness to take a risk, the way you don't care what other people think when you know you're right...that's what those kids need. What they deserve, Jackson. They need someone who believes in them."

"Of course, but—"

"Fuck them," she exclaimed, throwing her arms wide. "You trust your gut. You take risks. You know what's right. Do you know how much I would give to be able to say *to hell with it* and not feel like I was going to ruffle someone's feathers or upset someone?" She'd been a quiet kid, she hadn't been prone to tantrums or even giggling fits. It wasn't like she'd *never* wanted to belt out the lyrics to a favorite song or slide down the banister or put on her one and only sparkly crazy dress—a Halloween costume—and dance around the house. But she never did those things. Those things would not have been welcome in her house.

And it wasn't as if there wasn't a tiny part of her that had wanted to star in the school play and be the head cheerleader and get tipsy and dance with a cute boy in the back of a pickup at a river party.

Jackson encompassed all of the wild, live-life-big things that she'd always been on the fringe of, always jealous of, and now he was trying to squelch it.

It pissed her off.

"They're going to hear you." Though she noticed he was fighting a grin.

"I don't care. *I'm* saying fuck them."

And dang, it felt good. She'd never been much for swearing but, wow, there were times when fuck was *just* the right word.

Jackson pushed away from the counter and walked toward her. "Annabelle." His voice held a hint of warning.

She continued, the adrenaline coursing even faster with Jackson trying to quiet her. "And seriously, what has Scott ever done? So he's never done anything scandalous." She said the word with clear sarcasm. "He's also never done anything amazing. He's got to be the most boring guy I've ever—"

Jackson hauled her up on tiptoe by her upper arms and kissed her.

Probably to shut her up. But she didn't care. She didn't know if it was the adrenaline or the wine or Jackson, but the kiss turned carnal quickly.

Annabelle plastered herself against him, practically climbing up his body, her arms around his neck, her mouth open and hot under his.

He gripped her ass in both hands and lifted her against him, then set her on the countertop behind her. He stepped between her knees, her fitted skirt riding high. He cupped her head in both hands, taking over the crazy, out-of-control kiss.

After a moment, though, he gentled the pressure and drank her in.

She wriggled against him, but he had her trapped on the counter by his big body, her head in a gentle but firm hold.

Finally, she felt the agitated tension drain out of her and aroused tension took its place. She ran her hands up and down his arms, over his biceps to his shoulders, then up the sides of his neck to his hair. She moaned against his mouth and scooted forward, pressing her belly to his.

Eventually he let her lips go but rested his forehead against hers.

"Thank you," he said softly. "Thank you for believing in me. Thank you for the dinner party. Thank you for losing your mind for me."

She wanted to cry and laugh and kiss him at the same time. She wanted to wrap him up and take care of him. And how crazy was that? This big, tough bad boy needed the quiet, reserved English teacher to take care of him? But she thought that maybe he did.

"You okay if I let you go?" he asked. "No more Tasmanian devil impersonation?"

She shook her head. "No promises." If they were going to mess with him, she was going to get riled up. Period. And considering she wasn't sure she'd understood "riled up" until Jackson got to town, that was saying something.

He bent his knees slightly to look her directly in the eye. "I'm not caving," he told her. "But I need to take it easy, work into this. I'm not dropping the program, but I'm not going to push it right now."

"Every day you don't have that program going is a day a kid somewhere doesn't have that program in his or her life."

Jackson frowned, but she could tell it was because he hated that thought too.

"But if I push too hard and they resist and it takes *longer* to get it here, then we're hurting more kids, right?"

She pressed her lips together, the wheels in her head still spinning. "It's bullshit that they're not letting you do this right now," she finally said.

He grinned. "You're cute when you swear."

"Just do it. Please." She switched to pleading. That wouldn't be cute. "Set the farm up. That's who you are. You take risks, you push the boundaries, you go against the Bad grain—"

He stepped back and shoved a hand through his hair, his grin gone. "Dammit, I didn't just push the boundaries, I blew them up and scattered that shit everywhere. Don't you get it? I wasn't taking risks and being a proud rebel for a cause; I was stupid and headstrong and didn't respect myself or the people around me." He frowned down at her. "I have to take my time. I have to let them accept me. I have to prove myself."

"Why?" She slid off the counter, not wanting space between them. From this close, she had to tip her head back to look up at him. "Why do you have to prove yourself to them? Why do *they* have to accept you? What about me, and Coach, and Marc and Carter and Luke?"

His eyes were filled with a combination of frustration and affection. "Annabelle."

"What about me?" she repeated softly. "Isn't my acceptance enough?"

He took her by the upper arms again and looked into her eyes. "It's *all* about you," he said gruffly. "If I fuck up, and bring you down with me, I'll hate myself forever."

Wow. That was all good. She wanted to hug the words to her chest and cuddle them for a little while. But she didn't care about how his farm might affect her reputation or her relationship with the school board or even her job. Him standing up and saying that he was here and he was going to be part of this community, but that he was going to do it *his* way, was the right thing to do, and Jackson had taught her how good it could be to let go and act on emotion. "Don't be—"

"No," he said before she could go on. "No, dammit. Everyone loves you, everyone respects you. You can't put that on the line for me. It will be fine. It will. In time. I'll make it fine. But we have to chill the fuck out for right now."

She bit her bottom lip. This wasn't Jackson. His tendency was to go full steam ahead. She leaned back and he let go of her, stepping back and pulling in a deep breath.

"This is about Jenny isn't it?"

Jackson looked surprised for only a second. He nodded. "I'd like to think I can learn from my mistakes."

"You feel responsible for what happened to her." Frustration churned in Annabelle's stomach. He shouldn't still be paying for ten-year-old mistakes.

"Jesus, Annabelle," he said, raking his hand through his hair again. "I *was* responsible for what happened to her."

"But…" Annabelle's frowned. "You didn't—"

"I most definitely did," he said firmly, before she could go on. "I pursued her, seduced her, and assured her everything would be fine. I was so cocky, I really thought it would be. But we got caught and she was let go from the student teaching position and removed from the program. She sells real estate in Dallas now."

Annabelle said nothing for several heartbeats. She wanted him to know that he didn't have to tread carefully, bite back his first responses, take deep cleansing breaths continually through a dinner party. She'd been aware of his tension all night and everything he'd done, from the way he'd smiled to the way he'd held his fork, had seemed foreign and stiff.

"Fuck them, Jackson."

There was a hint of a smile at the corner of his mouth but he shook his head slowly. "This mouthiness is getting out of control."

"I don't care. I'm going to say how I feel."

He stepped in, an intent look in his eyes. "Now see, I can think of a lot sweeter things for that mouth to be doing than talking."

She smiled. Well, when he put it that way… She leaned toward him, anticipating his kiss.

He slid one big hand up her back and into her hair and brought his mouth close, but instead of kissing her, he put his lips near her ear.

"Get on your knees, Annabelle."

She tried to pull back, not sure if she'd heard him correctly, but he held her head.

"Good girls don't give blow jobs in the kitchen during a dinner party," he said. "But you will."

A shiver of desire went through her.

She wanted to. She was a little shocked by it, but it was true.

Acting on emotion, throwing caution to the wind—all of that seemed so obvious, so easy when she was with Jackson. And making this man—this tough, stubborn, hotheaded, loyal and noble man—feel good, however she could, was all she wanted.

Jackson would know that there was at least one person in this town who loved him exactly as he was and would do anything for him.

Her hands went to his fly immediately. His hands dropped to his sides and curled into fists as she unbuttoned and unzipped him. She pulled the front of his pants apart and his boxers down.

He was hard and ready. She took him in hand, stroking the length of his cock with the perfect pressure and speed to make him sway on his feet. She liked that a lot.

"Fuck. *Annabelle.*"

His groan made her shiver with pleasure and an unfamiliar-until-Jackson surge of feminine power go through her.

She went to her knees in front of him and took him in her mouth.

"Annabe—*fuck.*"

He grabbed the counter beside him with one hand, the other slid deep into her hair.

She ran her tongue from the base to the tip, then sucked again, harder.

He groaned and pressed closer. Annabelle moved a hand to his butt.

"What the hell are you two—" Michael stopped, the door still swinging inward.

Annabelle gave a little squeak and scrambled to her feet, turning her body to block Jackson's immodesty, pushing her hair back.

"Sorry," she said quickly. "We were…" Really? What was she going to say here?

Michael gave her a little grin. "I know exactly what you were doing." He didn't look offended. Slightly shocked, of course, but certainly not appalled. "Lucky bastard," he said to Jackson. "I'll tell everyone you're not feeling well and we need to clear out."

"No," Annabelle protested.

Michael's eyebrows went up. "Why don't you go in the bathroom and freshen up?" he said gently.

"No, I'm good. I—"

"You look like you were just giving a blow job," Michael said. "Your hair's a mess and your lipstick is smeared all over and your cheeks are flushed. Why don't you take a minute?"

She felt her cheeks heat further. She looked like she'd been giving a blow job. Maybe not the best way to face two people who were, for all intents and purposes, her bosses.

"Fine," she muttered, trying to smooth her hair down. She turned and headed for the opposite kitchen door and the tiny powder room off her foyer. When she looked into the mirror a minute later, she groaned. It was even worse than she'd imagined.

And still she was frustrated that they'd been interrupted. She didn't care who was in the next room.

She pressed a cool cloth to her cheeks, removed her lipstick and straightened her hair. Then she headed for the kitchen.

"Annabelle's amazing."

Jackson was talking to Michael and she hesitated outside the door, perfectly happy to eavesdrop on two hot guys talking about her being amazing.

"Daring, sexy, the kind of woman you never get out of your system."

Ooh, she liked that a lot.

"There is something about her," she heard Michael agree.

That was nice. But it didn't give her the thrill that Jackson's words had.

"But dude, she was on her knees in front of *you*. I can't ask her out."

Annabelle frowned. Ask her out? Michael?

"We're messing around," Jackson said. "She wanted a walk on the wild side. Turns out, she had it in her all the time. I just helped her find it."

Annabelle felt her stomach flip. Not in a good way.

For a moment her mind reeled as hurt and betrayal shot through her. But on its heels—*right* on its heels—was denial. Jackson might have a bad-boy reputation, but he was a good man. Even his scandalous affair with a teacher three years older than him had been about emotions. He was a risk taker; he might run his mouth, but he wasn't an unfeeling bastard.

In fact, one of his problems was that he felt *too* much.

It was one of the things she loved most about him.

Another thing was that he was devoted. That might be hard to see unless you were looking hard, but Jackson did the right thing.

When things had gone to hell in high school, he'd left town, but he'd still gone on to college, and not only made something of himself, but helped others. He hadn't gone for fame or money— he'd started a program to give other people direction, acceptance and support. When Coach needed him, he'd come back. When she'd needed him, he'd stepped up and showed her a whole new confident, powerful side that he'd seen long before she had.

So she knew exactly what he was doing right now. He was keeping up his end of their deal. She'd made him look good tonight and now he was making it up to her.

Tears stung her eyes.

"And she's got a thing for you," she heard Jackson say.

She felt a little dizzy. Had he really said that?

"What?" Michael asked. "Seriously?"

"Told me that upfront."

Annabelle hugged her arms against her stomach. Oh, god, this was about to be such a mess.

"Why didn't she say anything to me?" Michael asked

Jackson gave a bark of laughter. "She didn't know how to approach you."

"I never would have guessed her for a blow-job-during-a-dinner-party type of girl," Michael admitted.

"She didn't either until I came along," Jackson told him. "You're welcome."

It was stupid to think she could hear the tightness in Jackson's voice through the swinging door and across several feet of space, but she thought he sounded as though he was forcing the words out.

She pushed the door open and stepped inside. She focused on Jackson without even glancing at Michael. "I know what you're doing."

He sighed, realizing she'd overheard everything. "Annabelle—"

"This isn't what I want anymore."

"It's what you need."

Somehow she knew he wasn't talking about Michael. He was talking about her *not* having Jackson.

"I thought you'd changed," she said. "I thought you said you'd grown up."

"I did. I have."

"You stand up for the people you believe in," she pressed. "You'll do anything to make them happy, but you won't stand up for what will make *you* happy."

He said nothing. Just looked at her, a stubborn set to his jaw.

"I don't want to date Michael!" She glanced at him. "No offense."

Michael rolled his eyes. "Why would I be offended?"

She met Jackson's eyes again. "This isn't about you thinking I belong with Michael instead," she said. "This isn't about our deal. This is about you being afraid of letting people love you because you're afraid of letting them down."

Something flickered in Jackson's eyes at her use of the word "love". But yes, dammit, she was falling in love with him.

Michael, thankfully, stayed completely silent.

Jackson stood looking at her for a long moment, tension apparent in every inch of his face and body. Finally he said gruffly, "There are only two people in the world I've ever loved enough that I'd rather stay away than let them down. Coach. And you. I don't want to let you down."

Tears sprang to her eyes. He was falling for her too. That was amazing. And he was going to walk away from her because of it.

"So don't let me down now," she said simply.

"I don't think I can help it."

He turned on his heel and headed out through the kitchen door, through the still full dining room. A moment later she heard the front door open and shut.

She sagged against the counter next to her.

Several long, silent moments followed.

Finally Michael said, "So how about dinner tomorrow night?"

She lifted her head and looked at him. He wasn't grinning or flirting or coming on to her. "We're going to talk about Jackson the whole time, right?" she asked.

His expression was determined. "And this farm thing."

CHAPTER
TWELVE

HE REALLY HAD GROWN up and changed.

Jackson was proud of himself.

He hadn't run, he hadn't left Bad this time when everything went to shit. He didn't go to town and get drunk. He didn't pick any fights.

It was hard as hell.

Worse, though, was accepting the fact that he'd never get laid again. He'd never want another woman now that he'd had Annabelle.

But he also didn't go after Annabelle.

All he did was go to work on the ranch, bust his ass for long, hot, hard days, then go to bed.

And it was killing him.

He felt so ineffective, so *quiet*, so impotent—though he hated that damn word. Still it fit.

He wasn't *doing* anything and that was killing him.

He was biding his time, waiting for word about an interview with the school board, and tamping down any and every urge to ask someone about Annabelle.

Jackson was so lost in his thoughts that he almost didn't

swerve in time to miss the pickup truck that came barreling out of the north pasture as he was slowing down to turn in.

"What the fuck?" He slammed on his brakes and cranked the wheel to the right, getting out of the way as a second truck bounced over the end of the lane leading into the pasture and slid a little in the gravel, before straightening out and heading toward the ranch.

He'd caught a look at the driver and three passengers in the second pickup. Teenaged boys.

What were they doing out here?

Jackson turned into the pasture and went in search of liquor bottles and beer cans. But there was nothing. Tire tracks through the longer grass, a flattened spot where they'd apparently parked for a little bit. But there were no cigarette butts, nothing that had been used for target practice.

Frowning, he pulled his phone out and dialed Carter.

"Some kids were messing around in the north pasture," he said when Carter answered.

"I know."

Jackson scowled at that. "Did you also know they were driving like maniacs out on the road?"

Carter sighed. "I'll talk to them."

"You know who they are?"

"Yeah."

"What were they doing out here?"

Carter hesitated. "Uh, long story."

"I've got time."

"I'm at Coach's. Why don't you come up?"

Jackson wasn't sure he liked the sound of that. "Be there in five."

He went in through the back kitchen door as always. Carter was in Coach's living room, his feet up on the coffee table. Coach was in his recliner.

The man had collapsed again two days after Annabelle's dinner party. He'd been mucking out stalls in the barn—the idiot. Not even a full month after his heart attack. He'd taken ten years off his boys' lives—again—and he'd caught all kinds of hell for it. He'd been good for the past three weeks though. Of course, he'd been very rarely left completely alone for the past three weeks either.

"What's going on?" Jackson hadn't run off or started any fights, but he was sleep deprived and short on patience.

Carter looked over to Coach, who nodded.

Jackson frowned. "What's with the kids in the pasture?"

"Some of them were kids from here in Bad. They were showing the other guys around," Carter said.

"What other guys?"

"Kids from New Orleans. They're our practice run." Carter grinned. "The guinea pigs."

Jackson crossed his arms and tried to look hard-assed enough that Carter would quit being cute and tell him what was going on.

Carter rolled his eyes and got to his feet. "They're the first kids to come to the farm program. We decided to start with a few and make sure we've got everything in place. They're here for two weeks."

"What farm program?" But Jackson already knew.

"*Your* farm program," Coach said crossly from his chair. "Stop being stupid."

"I don't have a farm program," Jackson said evenly. His heart was pounding and he wasn't sure what exactly he was feeling in his gut but it was either excitement, or he was going to puke.

"Okay, you're right," Coach said. "Because sometimes you're kind of slow. But a pretty little English teacher here in town does."

None of that cleared up the excitement-versus-getting-sick thing at all.

"Annabelle did this?" he asked.

Carter nodded. "With some help."

"From you?"

"From all of us. Michael, Luke, Marc. Elyse. Coach."

Jackson dropped his arms and dragged a huge breath of air into his lungs. "What's going on?"

"I told you that if she says she's in love with you, you're supposed to believe her," Coach said. He sounded irritated.

Jackson frowned at him. Yeah, he'd said that. "Well, having amazing sex for the first time in your life has a way of making you think you're in love."

"Really? You never had amazing sex before Annabelle?" Carter asked.

He hadn't been talking about *him*. Had he? "Of course... No... It's complicated. It's different with her."

Coach chuckled.

Jackson was truly on his last nerve. He missed Annabelle. He missed her smile, the way her hair felt and smelled, her flowy skirts, the sweetness on the outside that hid the fire on the inside. And he didn't fucking feel like laughing about it. "Something you want to share, old man?" he asked Coach.

Coach wasn't fazed by Jackson's irritation. "Just that you didn't have amazing sex with Annabelle."

"Is that right? I don't remember you being there."

"At the risk of sounding cheesy and ruining your macho view of me," Coach said with a grin that said he didn't care one bit what the boys thought. "You made love for the first time. That has a way of messing with a guy."

Jackson looked at his mentor and friend. The man had been a father to Jackson in every way but biological. Coach had never said a word to Jackson that was untrue.

"You think I'm in love with her?"

"You are. And you know it, so let's get to the part where you go do something about it."

Jackson nodded. Fine, he could admit that much. "She deserves better."

Coach narrowed his eyes. He didn't like when Jackson put

himself down. "Then I guess you should be even more thankful that she's chosen you."

Jackson almost chuckled at the unexpected agreement. Almost. "Chosen me? I haven't seen her in three weeks."

"Whose fault is that?" Carter asked. "She's been down hanging out with everyone at Bad Brews, she's been going to yoga, you know where she lives."

"She's been to dinner with Michael." Jackson hadn't slept at all that night.

"Once," Carter agreed. "That was the night they came up with the plan for the program that they pitched to the rest of us the next day."

Jackson thought he should probably feel surprise rock through him. He didn't. He took a deep breath. "I'm *really* in love with her."

Carter nodded. "You're the only one who didn't know that three weeks ago."

Jackson hoped Annabelle knew it. But suddenly he couldn't wait to tell her. "Michael's not going to date her anymore," Jackson announced. "She's mine."

Carter gave him a smile and a you're-so-stupid shake of his head. "Michael never did date her. She's been yours since the day you walked into her classroom."

That was damn poetic for Carter but it still made Jackson's heart turn over. "Yeah," he said gruffly. "She has."

"You gonna wait 'til she comes out here tonight to talk about the farm stuff or are you going into town to tell her all of this?" Coach asked.

"She's coming out here?"

"Everyone's been meeting out here to get things going."

"Where the hell have I been?"

"Pouting." Carter grinned at him. "Nursing your poor broken heart. Of course it's your fault that it's broken, so that's really stupid."

"Fuck off." But Carter was right.

"By the way, I'm pissed you didn't ask me about using this ranch for part of your program," Coach said.

Jackson looked over at him. He took in the sight of the man who had always been larger than life, the man who had never held back anything Jackson had ever needed from him.

"Yeah," he finally said. "That was pretty stupid."

Coach just nodded.

"She's down at Brews with the girls," Carter said.

Jackson strode into Bad Brews fifteen minutes later.

Annabelle was sitting at her usual table with Randi and Regan.

Everything in him felt as though it was straining for her. His head was spinning with a million thoughts, his chest was tight with all of the things he needed and wanted to say, his entire body itched with the need to be against hers.

But he didn't go over to her. Instead, he crossed to the piano next to the little stage where live local bands performed from time to time and where, for whatever reason, Marc let people do karaoke on Tuesday nights.

He knew everyone was watching him. Conversation had completely ceased the minute he'd stepped into the bar.

He also knew that everyone in town knew everything that had gone on with him and Annabelle and the dinner party. They had to all know that Annabelle and the guys had put the program together—and that realization gripped his heart and made him stop for a second and breathe. They had to know that he'd been doing nothing but working for three weeks. And now here he was.

He knew they were expecting a big show. Something over-the-top from him. Jackson was a guy who stomped and raised his voice and made his presence known.

But there was only one person in here who needed to hear him.

He lifted the cover of the piano, put his hands on the keys... and played the first stanza of *Heart and Soul*.

No one said a thing, no one even moved.

He did it again, going as far into the song as he knew.

Then he turned, crossed his arms over his chest and met Annabelle's eyes across the room. "It's supposed to be a duet."

She nodded.

"I don't know how the rest goes without you."

She pressed her lips together. Her friends' mouths dropped open.

He thought that was a good sign. Hell, he hadn't even rehearsed.

"I hear you're starting up some farm program."

She nodded. "It's a brilliant idea, but the guy who came up with it is a stubborn ass. So I'm doing it."

He couldn't argue the *stubborn ass* part. "Some people in town don't want it."

"Nope. But the important ones do. Like all of our friends, and all of his teammates. And Coach."

He felt his throat and chest tighten. He wanted to cross that room and haul her into his arms. But he had more to say. "I'm in love with you."

She nodded. "I know."

"And I'd like to keep saying that...and acting on it."

A tiny curl to her lips. "I know."

"If you'll let me."

"People have had a hard time not letting you do what you want for most of your life," she said with a little shrug. "I don't see me stopping you now."

Happiness, heat, want, love, all hit him at once.

And she had a point about him always doing what he wanted.

So he crossed the bar, swept her up off the stool, and threw her over his shoulder. "Let's go."

She laughed, sounding a little breathless. Of course, that could have been because he had his shoulder digging into her diaphragm.

"Where?" she asked.

"Bed. For the next twenty-four hours. Tell your friends you won't be answering phone calls or texts."

"Whoa," Randi muttered.

Jackson grinned.

His grin grew even bigger when the bar erupted in applause as he started for the door.

He'd always loved making a crowd cheer.

He carried her out to the car and didn't let her slide—slowly—down his body until they were beside the driver's door.

When her feet touched the ground, he reached into his front pocket and withdrew the set of keys. It was his spare set, and he felt a little silly now, but he'd been in the gas station two weeks ago and had seen a keychain shaped like a big treble clef sign. He'd had to get it for her.

She noticed it immediately and her eyes filled with tears, but she smiled up at him. "My own set."

"You're the driver now."

Her eyes widened. "Oh yeah?"

"Anywhere you go, I'm right beside you."

She bit her bottom lip, her eyes sparkling. He expected something sweet or mushy but instead she turned and got into the car.

"Get in."

Laughing, he jogged around to the passenger side and slid in.

She turned the ignition and gave him a mischievous smile. "Hang on, Mr. Brady. You're about to have the ride of your life."

———

Thank you so much for reading Jackson and Anabelle's story! There's a lot more sexy, fun from Bad!

These books are all standalones and don't need to be read in any particular order!

The Best Bad Boy: (Jase and Priscilla)
A bad boy-good girl, small town romance

Bad Medicine: (Brooke and Nick)
A hot boss, medical, small town romance

Bad Influence: (Marc and Sabrina)
An enemies to lovers, road trip/stuck together, small town
romance

Bad Taste in Men: (Luke and Bailey)
A friends to lovers, gettin'-her-groove back, small town romance

Not Such a Bad Guy: (Regan and Christopher)
A one-night-stand, mistaken identity, small town romance

Return of the Bad Boy: (Jackson and Annabelle)
A bad boy-good girl, fake relationship, small town romance

Bad Behavior: (Carter and Lacey)
A bad boy-good girl, second chance small town romance

Got It Bad: (Nolan and Randi)
A nerd-tomboy, opposites attract, small town romance

Find all of my books at
ErinNicholas.com

And join in on all the FAN FUN!

Join my **email list!**
bit.ly/Keep-In-Touch-Erin

(be sure you get those dashes and capital letters in there!)

And be the first to hear about my news, sales, freebies, behind-the-scenes, and more!

Or for even more fun, join my **Super Fan page** on Facebook and chat with me and other super fans every day! Just search Facebook for Erin Nicholas Super Fans!

WANT MORE FROM THE BAYOU?

There's so much more from Erin's Louisiana bayou world!

Head down the road to Autre next and dive into the Boys of the Bayou series (where you'll first meet the Landry family)!

All available now!

My Best Friend's Mardi Gras Wedding

Sweet Home Louisiana

Beauty and the Bayou

Crazy Rich Cajuns

Must Love Alligators

Four Weddings and a Swamp Boat Tour

———

And be sure to check out **the connected rom com series,**

Boys of the Bayou-Gone Wild

Otterly Irresistible

Heavy Petting

Flipping Love You

Sealed With A Kiss

Say It Like You Mane It

Head Over Hooves

Kiss My Giraffe

———

And the **Badges of the Bayou** (where you get to know Michael LeClaire and JD Evans!)

Gotta Be Bayou

Bayou With Benefits

Rocked Bayou

Stand Bayou

Stuck Bayou

Just Wanna Be Bayou

———

And MUCH more—

including my printable booklist— at

ErinNicholas.com

ABOUT ERIN

Erin Nicholas is the New York Times and USA Today bestselling author of over forty sexy contemporary romances. Her stories have been described as toe-curling, enchanting, steamy and fun. She loves to write about reluctant heroes, imperfect heroines and happily ever afters. She lives in the Midwest with her husband who only wants to read the sex scenes in her books, her kids who will never read the sex scenes in her books, and family and friends who say they're shocked by the sex scenes in her books (yeah, right!).

Find her and all her books at
www.ErinNicholas.com

And find her on Facebook, Goodreads, BookBub, and Instagram!

Ingram Content Group UK Ltd.
Milton Keynes UK
UKHW011817230323
419066UK00005B/329